Magical Forest Musings

Susan Lavin and Patti Sapp

Copyright © 2020 Patti Sapp

ISBN: 9781735476872

Contents

Prelude

Twin sisters, Sonya and Sophie were separated for several years while they were away at school, each reaching goals, and starting their careers as young adults.

During this time, *I miss you*, was repeated frequently as they communicated by phone, text messages and video chats.

One frigid winter day Sophie shared with her sister a particularly challenging experience with her work in the fast-paced corporate world. As always, her sister did her best to lend a compassionate listening ear. Shortly after, Sonya petitioned, "Let's go away to someplace warm and tropical! We'll melt those blues away with the sunshine and refreshing beverages with little umbrellas."

Sonya and Sophie sat peacefully on a faded blanket watching the gentle waves glisten in the morning sun. It was their ritual this week, to walk down to the beach right before sunrise and share each new day. "I'm so grateful we decided to start this new tradition," said Sophie.

"Yes, now we have to start a list of all the destinations we'd like to visit on our sister's vacations," replied Sonya. "I think we should plan trips so we can visit every corner of the globe. We'll save all year long, then meetup and take a fabulous annual trip together." Both sisters nodded voraciously in agreement, and the tradition was born.

Rose Quartz

Sophie stood next to her mailbox when the new neighbor approached. "I'm Amanda from around the corner," the woman said, as if Sophie had been expecting her. Reaching into the pocket of her ripped jeans, Amanda presented Sophie with a glowing rose quartz. "It looks like you could use this," the petite lady offered. Sophie accepted the unexpected gesture of kindness.

"Oh my, thanks. It's beautiful. My name is Sophie." She was astounded by the perfection of this crystal, representing love. Sophie knew all about rose quartz and the ability to mend a broken heart. The neighbor continued her walk with a wave as Sophie held the gem in her hand.

Sophie was amazed with the fact that a total stranger would simply appear, gift her the exact crystal she needed, and then walk away.

Is this an example of an earth angel? Sophie wondered as her long legs took her up the gravel driveway. She held her mail in one hand and the rose quartz close to her heart.

This brief encounter marked the beginning of a friendship that neither woman realized was needed.

Amanda lifted Sophie's spirits on the exact day when she was in desperate need of that rose quartz. Carefully placing the rock in her pocket before she set out for her walk, Amanda thought, *I feel like this sweet gem is going to be rehomed today.* Divinely guided many times in the past, Amanda learned to simply comply when she felt her intuition inspire her.

How did my neighbor know this day, only a year ago, was the death of my best friend, my sister? Sophie sighed. The first anniversary has been more difficult than she anticipated. She awoke with a heavy heart. It literally felt like yesterday, rather than a year ago, that she had lost her dear friend.

Before her death, the sisters gallivanted through the wineries of Italy. Their life teemed with adventures and laughter back then. Their only concern during that trip was which restaurant they should select for dinner. They also had brief thoughts of spending too much money, which at the time, they agreed to ignore.

Still musing about Italy, Sophie entered her log cabin all alone, gently cradling the rose quartz in her hand. Her sweet kitty, Ginger, waited, instinctively knowing she needed company. Sophie placed the mail in the basket on the kitchen table. Moving into the living room, she crumpled upon the blue velvet loveseat and cried for the fourth time in just a few hours. Everything seemed to create tears. The heaviness of the day, even the kindness of a stranger, soon-to-be friend, resulted in a flood of emotion.

Sophie lost more than her twin sister on that same day last year; she lost a part of her soul, too. *My heart physically aches,* thought Sophie as memories washed over her. She cried herself to sleep in the middle of the afternoon, the new rose quartz clutched in her palm. As she had done many times before, Sophie allowed her dreams to fill with memories of better times.

In her dream, a sassy toddler smiled into a full-length mirror. Dressed in red gingham, with tiny dark curls sticking out in every direction, she eyed herself approvingly. She and Sonya were visiting their Grammy and Pop Pop's house, when Sophie declared, "Hi, Son-wah!" at the image reflecting back at her.

Grammy pointed, smiling in amusement, "Oh,

look, Sophie thinks it's Sonya inside the mirror!"

As Sophie recalled her Grammy, she also remembered her tiny poodle named Thumbelina. That little dog loved to lounge on Sonya's lap just for attention. The girls had been fascinated with the playful antics of that sweet pup, and Thumbelina had been the catalyst for their love of animals.

With eyes closed and a smile on her face, a memory dawned in her weary mind. Sophie chuckled aloud in her sleep as she thought of the first summer she and Sonya were trusted to walk to the local market to buy milk. It was only about a half a mile away, with just a few turns, but their ventures to the store made them feel very grown up. The sun shone as they skipped most of the way there, occasionally holding hands. Mr. Charlie welcomed them at the doorstep with a bright and cheery, "How are my favorite twin sisters today? Are you stocking up for your Candy Club again?"

"No, not today, we just need a gallon of milk," the twins chorused in unison, knowing they would be back to replenish their stash of sweets another day very soon.

The memory continued. "Wow, how can a gallon of milk seem so heavy?" exclaimed Sonya, as she passed the jug to Sophie for her turn to carry the cool, but somewhat slippery plastic container. Sometimes, they tried carrying it together, but this proved to be more of a comedy act, resulting in a fit of giggles. Sharing those simple tasks was part of their everyday life. The memory brought back strong emotions, especially on this day.

From the moment they were born, Sophie and Sonya had a mutual connection that went way beyond looking like two peas in a pod. Before they were even old enough to talk, the girls created a personal language, understood only by each other. With a giggle, glance, and simple sounds shared, they played together for hours, knowing exactly what the other was thinking. The two pudgy toddlers, with smooth, baby-soft dark skin and adorable black curls, were happiest when they were together.

Still dozing on the loveseat in her living room, Sophie allowed the thoughts of her twin sister to fill her heart for the remainder of this day.

Log Cabin

Sophie occupied the single log cabin in Duck Creek, nestled among a variety of farmhouses. From the outside, the cabin looked old-fashioned and cozy. For those who were lucky enough to enter Sophie's home, there were always gasps of "Oh, what a surprise!"

The inside of the modest dwelling overflowed with carvings, statues, and artifacts from all over the world. Sophie had been a world traveler from a young age. Many of the adventures had included her sister, Sonya.

Surrounded by relics and artwork from every corner of the globe, Sophie found herself settled into a quiet life. Her home was a true showpiece, like entering a world-class museum. She had a knack for artfully arranging her treasures, which far exceeded the price-value of the log cabin. For this reason, a state-of-the-art alarm system was installed when she had moved to the peaceful part of the community. Her property was backed by a verdant forest and bubbling river. Sophie often found herself entranced by the sounds of water and the swishing of the forest's trees in the wind, as she yearned for this tranquility away from the busyness of town.

Today, she sat mindfully with a mug of steaming tea, her eyes wandering in the distance of the green splendor. The surprise encounter had occurred just a week ago. *I already know Amanda and I will become close friends. I felt her warmth the moment she walked up to my mailbox.*

Sophie nestled comfortably on her blue velvet loveseat. On the table sat a bowl containing selenite hearts, several citrine gemstones, deep orange aragonite, and a variety of natural agates. Selenite was one of Sophie's favorites. Pure white gems that provided a sense of purity and cleansing. The gleaming pink of the rose quartz added a beautiful touch to her growing collection. *Is it possible the neighbor, Amanda, had the ability to look straight into my heart?* Sophie contemplated.

Sophie stirred the local honey into her tea mug and read the words of wisdom on the teabag. She bought this brand of tea because the messages always brought her insight and she found delight in reading the notes. The message tonight intuited, "Culinary delights create lasting relationships."

Sophie went to bed that night writing a grocery list in her head. She had sampled food from many corners of the earth and learned to recreate some of the dishes. The Mediterranean foods from the Greek Island, Santorini, would always be her favorites. She loved stuffed grape leaves, figs, and aromatic moussaka. Coming in a close second was the cuisine from West Africa, especially the fragrant fish soup made with sweet, fresh coconut. Cooking was therapeutic for Sophie. Sharing her creative and diverse dishes always brought deep satisfaction.

Sophie decided, *I'm going to invite Amanda over for lunch sometime soon.*

Right before drifting off to sleep, her dreams shifted to the kitchen of the home she had shared with Sonya, after they moved back to Duck Creek. It was right down the street from their jewelry boutique, Twins Silver Dream. The twins had favorite recipes they created together. They favored soups and stews during the winter months, always with homemade bread or muffins. Sonya loved to sample her vegetarian concoctions during that phase of her life. Later, they challenged one another to make the most unique burger in the world. Sonya had won that endeavor with her crazy homemade bison burger covered in hot peppers and secret spicy sauce. She boasted about that epic burger for weeks. Good memories of past times shared helped Sophie enjoy a restful night's sleep.

The Labyrinth

The next day Sophie woke up early, at peace and feeling hopeful. She headed through the forest on her property to her favorite spot near the river where she listened to nature and meditated.

On her way, she stopped at the labyrinth, always part of her morning ritual. The entrance faced the river, which was visible through the trees in the colder months. When she moved into her log cabin, it had been early winter. She spent hours and hours building the circular beauty, roping off her vision first, and changing it a few times until it suited her. Leather gloves, wool sweaters, and many Epsom salt baths later she fashioned the gravel portion of the labyrinth. Sophie estimated it took up about a quarter of an acre, but she wasn't particular about the numbers. She determined the progress has been worth the blisters and sore muscles.

In the spring she ordered flat rocks to complete her impressive project. This was a dream come true for Sophie. The trucks arrived and dumped forty tons of smooth rocks. She loved the shades of browns and grays and easily imagined the finished circular pathway. It was an exciting day, indeed. A single afternoon with leather gloves and a wheelbarrow demonstrated she wasn't going to complete the task alone. She was not one to shy away from hard work. However, the rocks were way too much for her, despite her capable body and toned muscles. She was a practical woman, though, and not easily discouraged.

After Sophie's attempt at manual labor, she was more appreciative of a little something special that she kept with her supply of handmade body oils. It was a small, but mighty jar of Tina's Salve, created by a talented friend and saved for occasions such as today. Made with dandelions and a variety of rich oils, Sophie massaged a generous amount onto her aching joints. *Hooray, I can feel the relief already,* she celebrated inwardly, slowly continuing the circular motions until every ache and pain gradually dissipated.

With the help of a local college, Sophie managed to find a team of strong students on their spring break that made her dream a reality. Four attentive and capable workers arrived at her log cabin each morning for several weeks. They were punctual and full of the kind of energy required for such a large project. "Just let us know where you want the rocks placed," one of the college workers said. They collaborated closely for hours, following directions easily. As the workers moved rock after rock, Sophie planted fragrant mint in the small spaces between the cracks and crevices.

They lifted and arranged the heavy boulders exactly as she instructed, for which she was grateful. By the end of the job, they had a congenial and easy working relationship. The workers appreciated the cash, of course, and the daily homemade treats and cool beverages made the breaks feel like a social gathering. The brownies and cinnamon raisin cookies flew off the plate each time they were offered. Sophie set out gallons of refreshing sun tea each day. She guessed the money she paid the college kids was used for more potent beverages in the evenings. *Oh, to be young again,* she smiled to herself.

"Why do you want a path that goes nowhere?" was a reasonable inquiry during one of the breaks. All four of the workers had thought this at one moment or another, but it was the first time any of them was brave enough to ask the question. Sophie secretly smiled to herself, delighted one of them was curious enough to ask the question.

Sophie took the time to explain her thoughts.

"It's a path I'll use for prayer and meditation called a labyrinth, an ancient symbol about becoming whole. I like to think it helps connect my body, mind, and spirit. My walks will represent a daily journey to my own center and back again out into the world." Her helpers listened politely as she continued. "The first labyrinth I ever saw was in France when I visited the Chartres Cathedral. During that trip, I also met a talented pastry chef who taught me to make the brownies I served today." Although her hard-working team didn't seem overly interested in Sophie's labyrinth description, the chat led to another generous supply of brownies.

That morning in the bright sunshine, Sophie stood at the entrance of her masterpiece, took a deep cleansing breath, and smiled. Setting an intention to receive peace and any other messages the Universe had to offer for her today, a passage from a favorite spiritual teacher swirled through her head.

> The mind can go in a thousand directions.
> But on this beautiful path, I walk in peace.
> With each step, a gentle wind blows.
> With each step, a flower blooms.
> ~Thich Nhat Hanh

The mint had grown quickly, as Sophie expected. For this project, the invasive plant was exactly what she needed. As she took purposeful, graceful steps around the pathway, she inhaled the uplifting aroma of the fragrant leaves. With no plan or time restraints, Sophie moved around the smooth pathway with quiet gratitude. She let her eyes soften just enough to see. It was a meditative journey for Sophie. She decided her walking meditation required her to become one with the moment but also one with the Earth. She placed each foot on the ground consciously. She felt the hard rocks resist against the soles of her feet. The beat of her own heart grew steadier and strong.

Sophie sat quietly in the center of the labyrinth, feeling calm and grateful. She reached up and held the pendant that was suspended by the sterling Bali chain. Sophie had chosen the glistening drusy to wear that day. It's a gem like sunshine. She now wore it close to her heart. Silent tears caressed her cheeks. She did not wipe them away. Sophie wanted to feel the love, as her thoughts drifted to Amanda and her newest crystal, the rose quartz. Her tears belonged in this precious moment.

A childhood melody the sisters had sung floated into her mind, as she sat still grasping the sunkissed stone. It was the sound of Sonya's sweet voice that came to her mind. She heard her sister singing, "You are my sunshine, my only sunshine. You make me happy when skies are gray. You'll never know, dear, how much I love you..."

Sophie smiled. "Sonya, I know you're here with me," she whispered gently.

Sunflowers

Sophie woke to the excitement of preparing a special meal for Amanda. Her gift of the rose quartz, and mere presence down the road from the log cabin, filled Sophie with hope. Hope of normalcy. Today's task was lunch.

The weather had turned cooler and Sophie gathered items from her pantry for soup. As she imagined the warmth and nourishment of a simple meal, a calmness with a touch of giddiness overcame her. It felt like the first day of school, the possibility of meeting a new friend. *What will Amanda think of my home filled with my collections?* she wondered. She smiled inwardly thinking of the silver bowl filled with natural gemstones, which now featured her new rose quartz.

The plan was to recreate the fish soup she had

enjoyed in North Africa. After mincing the garlic and onion, Sophie sauteed the ingredients in fragrant olive oil as her cabin began to feel more like home. Sophie hadn't been cooking lately, and she realized she had missed it. She prepared the broth in advance, adding the aromatic mixture of garlic, herbs, and onions. Later, when Amanda arrived, Sophie could add the potatoes and fish to complete the soup. Happy with her creation, she left the simmering goodness on the stove to set the table.

The simple meal would include Ksra, an African bread she started earlier that morning. The pleasant spice of anise seeds still lingered in the warm kitchen. It would pair perfectly with the fish soup.

Would it be weird to add a scoop of Ben & Jerry's alongside our dessert? she wondered. She couldn't remember the name of the sweet treat she enjoyed during that trip, but did recall exactly how it was prepared -- sliced bananas, tossed with a sauce of melted butter, orange juice, and a sprinkle of brown sugar, topped with shredded coconut. "Creme Brulee *Ben & Jerry's* would be so perfect alongside the bananas," she said to her kitty, Ginger, as she checked for an unopened carton in the freezer. Sophie felt hopeful and noticed, *I'm starting to feel hungry.*

Sophie decided to use the beautiful Morrocan pottery, which she had collected from that trip to Northern Africa. The community she had visited rejected the mass-produced ceramics that had become popular. Instead, they embraced the traditional, geometric designs. Bright orange and cheery yellow abstract linear images adorned the hand-shaped clay. Sophie selected the bowls, cups, and plates from her cabinet and arranged the table for two. *I'm sure I have candlesticks to match,* she thought as she reached up to the very back of the shelf. She finally managed to locate the candlesticks, which had never been used. The brand new candles were still in the box. *This is looking pretty. The autumn colors, with a warm glow of candlelight are beautiful* she noticed as she admired the table.

I wonder what type of music Amanda enjoys? Sophie pondered with curiosity. Near the table Sophie placed small speakers, barely noticeable, so she could listen while cooking. She selected sounds that made her move, called Berber music from Morocco. The rhythm was folksy and fun. Sophie recalled sitting in a small tavern, sipping a local brew, called Casablanca, while a live band played the lively melodies. That was the first time she had sampled the fish soup in a small village called Asilah.

I hope the soup brings Amanda the warmth and nourishment our budding friendship has brought me, was her thought as she ascended the staircase, heading for her bedroom to get dressed for her special visitor.

Sophie was ready, but had been daydreaming again, lost in thoughts, when she heard, "Hello, Sophie!" and saw Amanda poking her silver head through the front door.

"Oh, I didn't hear you knock. Come on in, Amanda!" Sophie called out as she glimpsed at Ginger, her timid cat, slipping away up the staircase. They rarely had guests, and her beloved tabby sought solitude.

Amanda entered the log cabin, extending her arm as she handed Sophie a beautiful arrangement of herbs, mums, and sunflowers tied with brown twine. A country arrangement filled with fragrance and color. "Amanda, these will look wonderful on the table with my pottery." Sophie headed to the kitchen to find a vase and placed the flowers in the center of the table. The added touch of the flowers and herbs completed the cozy atmosphere.

Amanda glanced at the gleaming spruce floors, the rich wool carpets, and carefully placed artifacts from around the globe. When Sophie returned to the entranceway, she noticed Amanda's wide eyes and laughed. "My home is deceiving from the outside. I know," she chuckled.

"Sophie, it looks like a fancy museum!" Amanda exclaimed. "It's obvious you've done all kinds of traveling. Wow. I feel like I've been transported to foreign lands simply by walking through your front door."

"Make yourself at home, please. Sit down and relax. Thanks, again, for the pretty flowers. Can I get you something to drink?"

"Thanks, Sophie. Do you happen to have something warm? There's a chill in the air this afternoon." Sophie brought out her basket of Yogi Teas. She offered the brightly colored packages to Amanda to choose from. "The purple Egyptian Licorice sounds intriguing."

"Yes, it has anise, the same flavor I've used in part of today's lunch. I think I'll have some, too," said Sophie as she poured the hot water into the colorful mugs, handing one to Amanda.

Sitting contently, sipping on the spicy tea, Sophie and Amanda softened their shoulders and relaxed into the blue velvet couch. The conversation turned to travels. Both women had done their share of visiting exotic places.

"Tell me about one of your most memorable trips, Amanda."

Amanda immediately thought of the Amazon excursion in the rainforest. She explained the extreme heat, the humidity, and the sheer beauty of the rainforest. "There were flowers literally as big as my head," she laughed. "I loved the colorful birds and learned so much on that journey," she recalled fondly. Mostly, I figured out that I could be independent and gained confidence by hiking and just exploring. I was only twenty-two and had recently graduated from college," Amanda reminisced.

"One of my favorite days on that trip was hiking through a sacred forest. It was a spiritual experience for me to be alone beneath the shade of a juniper tree. I found my true self on that trip, even though I didn't know I had been lost. I'm not sure if I'm making any sense at all!"

"That sounds awesome," Sophie said as she listened. "I went to the rainforest once, too. I'm trying to recall the name of the village. There was a Shaman there, a well-known man in those parts who everyone in my group was talking about. Some of the people I was with tried a weird herb drink called ashwagandha, or maybe it was ayihanga; something like that. I never heard how it went, because I decided to wander around the forest by myself on that day. I know what you mean about finding peace. It was a beautiful day for me. It's good to know we both found solace being in nature when we were younger. That's one of the reasons I love the trees on my property now and sitting near the river, especially," Sophie shared.

As they sat comfortably side by side, the newfound friends sipped the same tea, recalling memories of similar ventures. The timer on the oven interrupted their conversation as the smell of spicy anise wafted through the air. Sophie stated, "Ah, the bread is ready."

Leading Amanda to the kitchen, she took the loaf out of the oven and filled the bowls with fish stew. Amanda admired the table, realizing the flowers she brought were perfect. They continued their conversation like old friends. There was genuine laughter, even some teasing. It felt easy to be together.

"Umm, this is delicious, Sophie," Amanda said between bites.

Sophie told her about the tavern in Morocco where she had first tasted the fish stew, ending with, "Be sure to save room for dessert. It's a simple concoction I learned about on that same visit, but I'm adding my own twist," she revealed with a chuckle.

They agreed that dessert would have to wait a little longer, as they were both full, warm, and content.

"May I use your bathroom, Sophie?" Amanda asked as she got up from the table.

"Sure, right through the living room, at the top of the stairs, on the left," Sophie directed.

Distracted by the photos that hung along the

stairway as she climbed the steps, Amanda peered down at the colorful rugs and furniture in Sophie's living room. *This place is incredible,* she thought. When she reached the top, a painting stopped her abruptly in her tracks. A woman. The same face as Sophie. The large painting was so life-like, Amanda felt she was looking directly into her new friend's eyes. Yet, the hair was slightly different. Curls. The woman in the painting had short and deep brown curls surrounding the full cheeks and soulful eyes. Sophie had the same soulful eyes, but her hair wasn't as curly. *It must be a cousin, or perhaps her mother when she was younger?* Amanda guessed.

Sophie cleared the bowls and leftover lunch. She piled the used dishes in the sink and smiled. *Amanda is going to be a true friend. I can't believe we have so much in common. I'm so glad I finally invited her over. I'm loving having her here.*

Carrying more steaming tea along with the dessert to the living room, she settled herself on the couch as Amanda joined her. "What's your tea bag message?" Amanda asked.

Sophie replied, "Your greatest strength is love."

"Yes, that's a good one. I love this brand; it's been my go-to for years," Amanda revealed. "During the pandemic I used the messages to guide me sometimes. Those times were strange, weren't they? Was that whole COVID thing happening when you moved here, Sophie?"

Amanda glanced over at Sophie and realized she had become quiet. The silence was deafening. "Are you alright?" she asked.

"Yes, I lived here during the COVID pandemic, but not in this cabin. My sister and I owned a brownstone townhome down on Main Street, not far from Bryan's cafe," she said with a slightly altered, careful tremble to her voice.

Amanda heard sorrow in Sophie's statement. She saw Sophie's back stiffen and felt a sudden chill. Amanda's mind began to wander. *The painting. It must be her sister. I wonder if she moved away?*

Sophie finished Amanda's thought, "My sister, Sonya, died of the virus. It's been a little over a year now. The day you walked by and handed me the rose quartz, that was the anniversary of Sonya's death. She was my twin sister," Sophie added.

As if they had known one another for years, Amanda offered Sophie an embrace. Afterwards, the two women sat in a comfortable silence.

Eventually, their time together came to an end as the tea grew cold. There would be many more conversations, shared desserts, and warm tea for these new-found friends.

Drunken Cow and a Poodle

"My throat hurts," said Sonya.

"You always take a day or two to recuperate from flying, and the plane was more crowded than usual," replied Sophie. The heavy, overfilled suitcases were still in the corner of the living room, lying sideways, and slumped over, just like Sonya, even after more than a full night's sleep. "Uumm, the Uber dropped us off at seven, and we were both snoozing by 7:30. By the way, you were snoring like a drunk cow last night!" laughed Sophie.

"We don't have to rush to unpack. Let's just take our time to relax and recuperate from the jet-lag. The store is in good, capable hands," Sophie reminded her sister.

Before leaving for the jewelry buying trip to Italy, they made certain their Twins Silver Dream boutique was ready for customers. The young girls, who usually worked weekends for Sophie and Sonya, agreed to keep the boutique open during the busiest part of the week, too. They were very dedicated and enthusiastic about the jewelry, and quite frankly, would have been pleased to be paid in gemstone rings and earrings. "Devin and Lily spend the majority of their paychecks at Twins Silver Dream anyway," admitted Sonya, "We should just let them pick out a selection of the new jewelry when it arrives."

Sophie and Sonya always made sure the sterling was brightly polished and the display cases were filled with one-of-a-kind earrings, pendants, bracelets, rings, and necklaces. The beautiful pieces were created especially by talented jewelry artisans from across the globe. The showcases resembled a rainbow, and regular customers loved to browse, knowing that they would always find a new piece to cherish. "It's going to be so fun to see Giovanni and Aziza in person at their studio, instead of just on FaceTime," Sonya acknowledged as they locked up the back door to the shop one last time before the big trip to Italy.

Later in the morning, with their favorite Polish pottery mugs filled to the brim with robust coffee, they headed outside and sat on the porch swing. They sat side by side, wrapping themselves in the wool blankets they kept for cool mornings. "I absolutely loved our trip, but I also love being home," admitted Sophie. The sisters had decided a few years earlier to move back to their hometown and buy a brownstone together. Their home was cozy and incorporated both their personalities. They glanced skyward at the same time, as a couple of bright bluebirds flew from branch to branch, cheerfully singing a morning song.

"Those white, puffy clouds remind me of a day when we were little," reminisced Sonya. "Do you remember lying on our backs and finding animals in the sky?"

"Oh look, there's a sheep over there," laughed Sophie. "And a poodle with her little ones on the other side, right over the bare branches of the maple tree!"

The early sun was shining down, glistening on the dew that gathered on the leaves of the holly bushes. The shiny, red berries waved a soft, "welcome home" in the gentle breeze.

"The warm, soothing coffee feels good on my throat," Sonya remarked, as the swing swayed in harmony to nature's music. The fluttering tree branches rustled with squirrels happily playing and chasing each other.

Sophie walked into the kitchen to refresh their coffee and pop a few cinnamon rolls into the oven. Whenever the sisters baked, they doubled the recipe and froze some for later. This ritual was a blessing today. After a month in Italy, they cherished the baked goods stored in their freezer. Sophie cracked open the kitchen window, so she could hear the oven timer go off.

"I'm glad that most of our treasures will be shipped," said Sonya. "Not a single thing would have fit in my bag without the zipper popping open."

Both Sophie and Sonya reached up and caressed their new necklaces at the same moment. "Afterall, the trip was a buying trip. We really were supposed to buy for ourselves. We are walking advertisements for Twins Silver Dream, right?" chuckled Sonya.

Sophia had chosen a big, bold lapis pendant with delicate silver wrapped in a swirling design across the deep blue gemstone. Sonya loved her purple amethyst druzy pendant, shaped like a teardrop. It sparkled in the sunlight and created rainbows everywhere. They both chose vintage-looking Bali chains that laid close to their hearts.

"Yum!" said Sophie as the delectable aroma of cinnamon wafted out onto the porch.

"Huh?" said Sonya, watching her sister get up to take the buns out of the oven as the timer dinged.

"Can't you smell the cinnamon? Remember, we splurged on the special Madagascar cinnamon at the market in town?"

Sonya looked perplexed and stated, "I don't smell anything, but my stomach is grumbling. The last thing we ate was popcorn we picked up at the airport. It did go quite well with the bourbon and ginger ale on the flight, as I recall."

They sat outside for a little longer, still cozy in their blankets, enjoying the delectable rolls. Independently, their thoughts drifted to various aspects of the amazing trip. The twins truly enjoyed each other's company whether traveling across the ocean on exciting adventures or sharing a simple, quiet morning lounging on the porch.

Sonya's eyes were feeling heavy, and she suddenly started to doze off. Sophie quickly scooped up her sister's mug before it slipped out of her hand.

"Whoa, I feel so tired. I think I'll go back to bed for a bit," Sonya lumbered towards her room exhausted, even though she slept for over twelve hours the night before.

Sophie hummed an Italian tune stuck in her head as she cleaned up the coffee mugs and breakfast dishes. She didn't feel tired at all, but was looking forward to getting back to the boutique and sharing all of the stories with their favorite customers. *We may have to add a few new cases by the window,* laughed Sophie at the extravagance of their buying spree.

"Are you ready to get up yet, sleepy head?" Sophie joked, peeking her head into Sonya's room. "You've been asleep for most of the day!"

Sonya was still drowsy and her throat felt like razor blades each time she swallowed. "I was just going to rest for a few minutes," not immediately realizing that it was dusk and that she'd been fast asleep since breakfast. "The long plane ride really must have done a number on me this time," Sonya mumbled. Trying to sit up, she whispered more to herself than Sophie, "My throat is so dry. I feel kind of hungover."

Sophie smiled at her sister and said, "Well, let's get you some water, and if you are hungry, I saved you some salmon with dill sauce and jasmine rice. I didn't try to wake you. I thought you needed the extra rest, sleeping beauty."

"I'm not even a little bit hungry, but could drink a gallon of warm tea," murmured Sonya. She had only made it to the side of her bed when she concluded she was too dizzy and weak to stand up. "Sophie, I feel terrible."

"Maybe you are getting the flu? Do you feel warm? Let me go find the thermometer," answered her sister.

Sophie went to their shared bathroom and rummaged through the medicine cabinet. She didn't find a thermometer but did locate some Advil. "This should help your sore throat," she told Sonya. "Maybe the thermometer is in the junk drawer," she hoped, reaching into the cabinet next to the kitchen sink. "I found it," she announced, walking back into Sonya's room. "I can't remember the last time we needed the thermometer," said Sophie.

Sonya was still sitting on her bedside, eyes glazed and watery. Sophie observed her sister's flushed face. She had a crease from her temple that ran all the way down to her chin from sleeping on a fold of her wrinkled pillow.

"Let's see if you have a fever," Sophie said as she handed the thermometer to her sister. It showed 99.2. "No big deal, just low grade," said Sophie. "Hopefully, after some tea and Advil, you'll be feeling fine. I can't wait to plan our day at our jewelry boutique for tomorrow. I've missed all the smiling customers and the way we made the place feel comfortable and inviting. I don't think we've ever been away for this long."

Dr. Shirley

Their unpacked luggage was still lying in the hallway, and it looked like it would stay there a little longer.

Returning from overseas and jet lag were finally catching up to Sophie. After reading in her favorite well-worn tapestry chair for a tad, she decided to call it a night. "I'm going to take a bubble bath and go to bed. Sweet dreams."

Sonya nodded in reply and said, "I can't seem to keep my eyes open, so I'm going to bed early too. My throat feels a little bit better, but I feel so run down. Everything aches."

Sophie awoke with the birds the next day and started unpacking. She was on her second load of laundry when she finally heard Sonya, "Sophie, I need help. I'm so dizzy, I don't think I can stand."

Sophie rushed in and found Sonya somewhat disoriented, still wearing her rumpled clothes from the day before. As she wrapped an arm around her sister's waist to help her up, Sophie could tell she was weak. "You are burning up, and your clothes are soaked!" They made it the corner of her bedroom where Sonya collapsed onto the loveseat. Her coughing suddenly became violent, and she gasped for breath. Each time she began to talk, the coughing would start again.

"I think we should call Dr. Shirley," said Sophie. "You may have picked up a bug on the plane."

"I just need to rest today. I'll be fine," replied Sonya, trying to smile and keep it light. Although she had no desire to get off the loveseat she knew a quick shower and fresh pajamas would make her feel better.

Afterward, Sonya felt worn out. Another dose of Advil, and her body relaxed under a mound of warm blankets while she drifted back to sleep.

The next morning, the throbbing in Sonya's head pounded to the point she couldn't focus or move her eyes. The coughing was excruciatingly painful and she gasped, "I can't catch my breath."

Sophie called their friend and neighbor, Dr. Shirley. "I know your office hours haven't started yet, but Sonya is really sick. Maybe it's the flu or pneumonia? Can you catch pneumonia on a plane?"

Dr. Shirley said to meet her at the office in an hour. It took Sophie the entire hour to help Sonya dress in sweatpants and a T-shirt and slip her feet into fuzzy slippers. "I don't care what I look like, as long as she can stop this coughing," Sonya said in between fits of near-choking. "My chest and side ache even worse than yesterday."

As they pulled up to the small cottage where their friend practiced general medicine, they saw Dr. Shirley. She had just parked her trusted, little red Volkswagen beetle, a car she'd been driving forever. "Here, let me help you inside," gently grasping Sonya by the elbow and quickly winding her arm around her shoulder, with Sophie on the other side. "You are really weak."

Dr. Shirley performed her routine examination, and Sonya broke out into fits of gasping and coughing, holding her side. "Why does my chest hurt so much?" she questioned in between coughs.

"I think you fractured a rib. Have you been coughing this much all night?" asked Dr. Shirley.

Sonya couldn't even answer the question, but Sophie said with worry in her voice, "Yes, she's had coughing fits all night. However, when I checked on her, she was mostly asleep through even the worst ones."

Dr. Shirley concluded Sonya had a nasty case

of pneumonia. She thought certain with an anti-biotic, aspirin, and a strong cough prescription that Sonya's 102 fever would go down and the coughing would ease. "Unfortunately, the rib will have to heal on its own. I know it hurts, but the anti-inflammatory should help, and once your coughing subsides, it will heal."

"Thanks for seeing us right away. We owe you lunch at Bryan's Cafe sometime soon," said Sophie as she helped Sonya back into the car.

Sophie took Sonya back home and got her settled on the couch. "I feel so much better now that we've seen the doctor. I'll run to the market and pick up some healthy fresh fruits and vegetables and get your meds. You look like you need to just sit and relax." Sophie put on some soothing meditation music and made sure Sonya had plenty of blankets and pillows to prop her up. The coughing seemed to lessen if she was sitting rather than lying down.

As Sophie roamed the aisles of the market, she made a mental list of ingredients she would need to make fresh bread and a big pot of vegetable soup. *Soup seems just the thing for Sonya to knock this pneumonia out of her system.* She also bought a fresh chicken, thinking that a combo of chicken noodle soup and lots of veggies might be even better. *Chicken soup cures everything, right?*

Sophie filled up her basket with tangerines,

asparagus, carrots, onions, celery, and a head of purple cabbage that caught her eye on the end display. She grabbed fresh thyme and basil, thinking they would be great in the soup. *An apple a day keeps the doctor away,* came to mind as she picked out several small Pink Lady apples. *Too late for that, but it can't hurt to start eating them now,* she thought optimistically.

Sophie also needed yeast, eggs, flour, and their favorite, a variety of cheeses. After all, they pretty much cleared out both the pantry and refrigerator before leaving for Italy.

Baking fresh, rustic bread was on her agenda for the day, while the savory soup simmered on the stove. *Better pick up some Irish butter to go with the bread,* she thought, while she headed towards the other side of the store.

Meandering down to the dairy case and remembering the almond milk, Sophie scooped up a few small pints of Ben & Jerry's to cheer up Sonya when she started to feel better. Peanut butter swirl and chocolate chip mint were two of her top choices.

As she turned the corner, there was Devin, one of the girls taking care of their Twins Silver Dream jewelry boutique. "Hi, Sophie. Welcome home! We loved all your text messages and updates on your trip. The new jewelry sounds totally amazing, and Lily and I can't wait to see it!" Devin said in her sing-song voice. "The customers missed you and Sonya, but after showing them the newer pieces, we had them leaving the store with their hands happily filled with treasures. We are going to need to restock all those empty cases!"

Devin was smart and articulate, and the customers loved her energy. Lily was more mellow, with a calming manner that put customers at ease while they browsed. Both girls were passionate about jewelry and learned about the gemstones, where they are mined, and the long and varied list of qualities each type of stone holds. These assets made communicating with new and regular customers a plus, and Sophie and Sonya were fortunate to have competent employees that had also become dear friends.

As she checked out, a few other friends passed by, but Sophie just gave a quick wave and headed out the door. She had been gone longer than expected and wanted to get back to the house quickly to check on Sonya and get her meds to her. *Next time, I'm going to make a list,* she told herself. *I sound like a broken record.. I always think making a mental list will work. I have a great memory for facts and figures, but somehow with grocery shopping, I sometimes forget things. Sigh.*

As she pulled their bright blue Mini Cooper into the driveway, Sophie had a good feeling that with Dr. Shirley's care, and the new medicine, her best friend and sister, Sonya, would be back to her positive and happy self very soon.

Sophie unpacked the groceries in only a few trips, carrying as many totes as possible, even though they were heavy and practically overflowing. *I can fit one more bag around my left wrist.* she encouraged herself, as she chuckled, always trying to outdo her personal best of six bags at once.

With no time to waste, Sophie started on the bread first, since the dough took a while to rise. Next, as the chicken roasted in the oven, she started peeling and chopping in preparation for the soup.

Sonya had a spastic, coughing fit as she padded softly into the kitchen still wearing her cotton sweatpants and fuzzy slippers.

"Oh, here's your medicine," said Sophie. "I was in such a hurry to start cooking, I forgot to bring it to you."

"Thanks, I just woke up when I heard the rumble of Blueberry pulling into the yard." Blueberry was their cute little car's affectionate nickname. They decided and agreed on the name almost immediately after buying the car together. Living in a small town, they walked to most errands, and only needed a car for longer trips or major shopping.

As the hearty, healthy soup simmered and the

bread began to get brown and crusty, the aromas in their small townhouse made Sophie hungry. She set the table with their colorful Polish pottery dishes and got the butter out to soften.

Sonya peeked inside the large pot and remarked how good the soup looked, but said, "I'm surprised I can't smell it."

After only two days, the meds seemed to be working; Sonya was alert, her fever down, and the coughing much improved. Her side was still quite painful, and the broken rib would take much longer to heal. "At least my hacking isn't making it worse now," wrote Sonya, when Dr. Shirley texted her for an update.

Sparkle and Shine

Sophie was pleased to spend most days back in the Twins Silver Dream boutique, where the gemstone jewelry made her smile. It almost felt like play, rather than work, polishing the glass cases, rearranging the beautiful artisan-created jewelry to make sets that coordinated, but weren't cookie-cutter matchy. *I can't imagine ever buying a couch, chair, curtains, and pillows in all the same fabric,* she considered. *I'm so glad perfectly matching jewelry sets are no longer trending. I never understood that at all,* she admitted.

Sonya was still recuperating from pneumonia and had orders from Dr. Shirley to rest and heal for at least another week. However, she gave her sister ideas and opinions. She was on her second round of antibiotics and cough suppressant and was hopeful to have her energy back soon. "I think we should place the new glass case under the window, for maximum sunlight, so the jewelry from Italy will really sparkle," suggested Sonya at breakfast that morning.

It's a good sign that Sonya is interested, thought Sophie. *She must be finally on the mend.* "I like that idea." she replied to Sonya.

Sonya started taking walks to regain her strength, but noticed her ankles and knees were not cooperating. "I've never had pain just taking a stroll around town," she said to Sophie. "Geez, I feel like an old lady! Maybe I should exercise more."

The weeks drifted by quickly, and soon the sunshine was consistently warm and the peonies blooming. "Fresh flowers on the kitchen table remind me to appreciate the little things," smiled Sonya as Sophie nodded in agreement. Her aches and pains were getting better, or at least they were becoming routine, and she learned to live with the old-lady knees and occasional chest discomfort. Life was getting better.

Sophie contacted the Italian delivery service for the second time that week, in hopes of learning what was taking their precious gemstone jewelry so long to arrive. The entire country of Italy was in lockdown, with COVID-19 cases soaring to every corner of the land. The mail delivery was in a gridlock, with workers quarantined or hospitalized.

The global pandemic was spreading everywhere.

Luckily, local artisans were still working and creating the one-of-a-kind jewelry popular at Twins Silver Dream. They were not going to run out of jewelry, but still eagerly awaited their shipment. Picking out jewelry was always fun, but actually receiving it was like Christmas morning every time. They anticipated unwrapping each piece and tried to guess which customer it was best suited for. Most patrons had a personal sense of style and preferred certain gemstones and colors. "Our predictions are usually right," they admitted and boasted just to each other.

"Cheryl loves larger, bold pieces," stated Sophie.

"And Val almost always chooses shades of blue, especially stones that sparkle," chimed in Sonya.

"It's surreal to realize we missed the coronavirus outbreak just in time," said Sophie.

"Our trip was amazing and filled with adventure, long walks through the vineyards, and so many wine tastings, we lost track," Sonya responded. "And to think I wasn't a fan of red wine before the trip," as she sipped on a blend of cabernet with undertones of spicy nutmeg. They were enjoying happy hour out on the porch with a charcuterie board complete with prosciutto, smooth-smoked gouda, creamy goat cheese, a variety of crackers, grapes, and raspberries.

"Should we make this dinner and just eat ice-cream later for dessert?" suggested Sonya. Healthy living was a priority for them but on occasion, "balance," which almost always had something to do with Ben & Jerry's and chocolate, was in order.

"Well, Happy Hour was dinner, so let's keep the celebration momentum going and use our new dessert spoons for the ice cream tonight!" Sonya said with a gusto she wasn't quite feeling. During their trip, they bought matching sets of very ornate spoons engraved with, Always have dessert first. "Maybe we will have our ice-cream first the next time." she added.

Sacred Heart

Even during a pandemic, business was booming and the sisters decided to finally take a day to themselves to regroup and relax. Their little town had yet to be hit by illness. The news continued to report all kinds of devastation in neighboring cities. Other than social distancing and mask requirements, they had not been impacted by COVID-19.

It was close to Mother's Day. Lily and Devin liked to remind the masked customers, "Jewelry makes a wonderful gift." The two dependable employees were now working full time at the boutique, right next to Bryan's Cafe, where they were frequent customers. Lattes and croissants were an excellent reward for bringing smiles to the customers' faces. It was not a partnership, per se, but the staff at Bryan's often referred people to the twins, and vice versa.

"Today will be fun. I'm happy we finally invited Dr. Shirley to join us for lunch. She's meeting us here at the house around one this afternoon. She only has patients this morning, so it works out with her schedule. We can all go to Bryan's Cafe together," said Sophie to Sonya. Sonya gave a brief nod to let her sister know she was listening.

"I can't believe it's been so long since I practically carried you into her office that chilly morning. That was a scary day," declared Sophie. "It's about time we paid back her kindness."

"I'm taking Blueberry over to the post office to make certain no packages were delivered for us," said Sophie. "Are you being lazy again today? You aren't even dressed," she teased her sister.

As soon as Sophie headed out the door, Sonya collapsed back on the couch and curled into a ball. *I can't believe my chest is aching again and my head is pounding.* Tears started rolling down her cheeks. She was exhausted from putting on a bright face and not complaining to Sophie. Constant fatigue and achiness that had been a part of her life for months was getting old. *Some days, life is good, and I feel almost energetic,* she rallied, *but not today.*

Sonya drifted into a deep sleep, once again bundled up with blankets, her body shivering in icy coldness. It was a warm sunny day outside, but she was still freezing even piled with blankets.

Dr. Shirley announced herself as she stepped onto the porch, "So-nya! So-phie! Where are you?" Nobody answered, so she relaxed on the swing knowing she was a few minutes early. Dr. Shirley noted the little blue car wasn't out front and assumed they would return home soon. She was in her own little world, thinking about Bryan's shrimp salad, when she heard a faint groan and a weak "help" coming from inside the house.

The door to the quaint brownstone was open, so she went inside hoping she was imagining the soft cry. As she entered the living room, she heard it a little louder. "Help!" This was real, and somebody was in trouble. Her training as a doctor kicked into full gear and she ran down the hall towards the voice. Sonya was tangled in sweaty sheets and blankets, thrashing around the bed, her hair matted in clumps where she usually had soft curls. Sonya looked delirious and didn't fully comprehend that Dr. Shirley was even in the room. "I'm here," she tried to comfort her friend. Sonya was not responding, but now just laid there limp, drenched and unresponsive.

"I'm calling 911!" Dr. Shirley blurted out, even though she was alone in the nightmare situation.

With sirens blaring, the professionals rushed inside to take charge. They were covered from head to toe in protective gear. Dr. Shirley was composed as much as the scene allowed, but was thrown by the appearance of their PPE. She haltingly explained, "I'm her doctor and friend. I found her like this and called for help. Sonya presents with a high fever, apparent dehydration, and is no longer responsive. She had what I thought was pneumonia a few months ago, but this is way beyond that. She needs to go to the hospital immediately."

As the medical team worked quickly to put Sonya on the stretcher, Dr. Shirley heard her friend barely whisper, "Sophie."

Dr. Shirley was shaken, but still jumped into the back of the ambulance with her mask on, as both a physician and friend. They pulled away, as the two competent paramedics took Sonya's vitals and tried in vain to get fluids hooked up. She was so dehydrated that they were not successful in finding a strong vein.

Dr. Shirley heard Sonya call out weakly, "Sophie, I can't…" as she moaned.

Grabbing her phone, she dialed Sophie's number. When Sophie answered, the doctor could not make the words come. Dr. Shirley was shaken to the core, and it took her an extra minute to calm her voice enough to stutter. "I'm, I'm, on, on my way to the hospital with Sonya. Come, come quickly!" Dr. Shirley's hand shook and she accidentally dropped the phone. It slid sideways underneath the stretcher, as they careened around a bend in the road. The paramedics were too busy to even notice, and there was no way to successfully retrieve it until later. She knew Sophie would know to rush to Sacred Heart Hospital, as it was the one and only medical facility in the area.

They pulled into the emergency entrance for ambulances and everything happened quickly. A bigger team of personnel was waiting and jumped into action. Their professionalism was apparent, and the teamwork showed this was becoming routine. They worked seamlessly to bring out the stretcher with the oxygen mask still attached. Sonya was still, except for her head moving back and forth with raspy coughing.

Out of the corner of her eye, Dr. Shirley recognized the little blue Mini Cooper as it skidded to a stop behind the ambulance. She ran to Sonya's twin sister and the flood of tears she'd been holding inside burst out. She couldn't stop her raw emotions, not even to explain what happened. Sophie trembled, "How? What?" unable to make her thoughts into a sentence. The two friends clung to each other in silence for several moments.

It was clear they were not allowed inside where Sonya was being examined. Suddenly, a friendly, but competent nurse appeared and introduced herself as Ms. Janice Prahl. She handed over a clipboard, a sterilized pen wrapped in plastic, and two bottles of water. "Please sit over here and fill out these forms. I will go check on the patient and come out with updates as soon as I can. Are there any pre-existing conditions we should know about right now?" she asked gently.

"No, it's my sister, and she's healthy and was very strong until her bout with pneumonia a few months ago," Sophie answered.

"Be careful. She broke a few ribs from coughing, and they are still not totally healed," added Dr. Shirley.

Meanwhile, Sonya was being treated with utmost care and consideration inside a clean and sterilized cubicle. They bypassed the triage area and took her immediately to the COVID-19 hall of the hospital. Her symptoms were high fever, dehydration, and persistent coughing.

After an examination, it was determined Sonya was required to have the nasal swab to make an accurate diagnosis. Sophie was in and out of consciousness at this point, but awake enough to push the technician away and blurt out, "EECH, STOP," as the very long swab invaded her nose.

By the time Sophie finished the forms, which were barely legible due to her shaking hands, the nurse walked towards them. "Your sister has been admitted into the COVID section of the emergency room. We are waiting for the lab test results. All quarantine precautions are being taken, and they've just given her some medication through the IV to calm the coughing and reduce the fever. We have an excellent team of doctors here at Sacred Heart, so she is in very good hands," Nurse Prahl tried to reassure them.

Meanwhile, a young woman was pacing nearby with a baby girl on her hip. She also had a toddler sitting on the ground playing with a plastic dinosaur. The mom was attempting to keep her baby happy, while filling out forms. You could tell her stress level was high, as she shifted the sweet girl from side to side, saying in a gentle voice, "I know sweetpea. I want Daddy to come home, too."

The same nurse came out, but veered towards the young family instead of Sophie and Dr. Shirley. Suddenly, mournful crying accentuated the tense outdoor space of the hospital.

"But I heard a White House official say on the news that if you are young and healthy, it will be just like a mild flu," she sobbed.

Staying professional, but obviously extremely shaken, they overheard the nurse ask, "Is there anyone I can call for you, Mrs. Sanchez?"

Meanwhile Sonya was in acute respiratory distress, and the doctor needed to intubate ASAP. There was no time to call an anesthesiologist to sedate her. Being intubated with an endotracheal tube placed in the nose and threaded into the airway is not a pleasant experience under any circumstances, but with no anesthesia, intubation is excruciating. Sonya was awake, but not alert, so she didn't know what was happening. She was fairly comfortable, with the calming medication already in her system. Then, the technicians positioned Sonya on her stomach, facing towards the floor. "Watch her ribs," reminded one nurse. The gasket portion was inflated to hold the ventilator tube in place.

The chief physician, Dr. Betsy Phillips, explained, "Now the machine will breathe for you. Try to relax and don't fight it, Sonya."

Within minutes, Sonya's dark skin had a sweaty sheen, and her arms and legs started shaking. Spastic, choking sounds could be heard down the hall as her body convulsed at the same instant the machines sounded an alarm. "Code blue, code blue," resounded clearly through the ER where Sophie and her friend paced just outside the door.

Sophie froze. She knew.

Delivery

Moving out into the country to the log cabin had been one of the best decisions Sophie had made. She sat on the front porch sipping her morning coffee. It was quiet and serene. *This would be about the time we'd be going to our jewelry boutique,* she thought absent-mindedly. She had closed the doors to Twins Silver Dream over a year ago. Packing up the boutique was a distant memory. It had been a painful time. One foot in front of the other. Numb most of the time.

The house the twins shared in town sold quickly.

The basement of her log cabin was filled with the cardboard boxes and jewelry display cases from the business. Evidence of hard work and entrepreneurship were nothing more than carefully labeled boxes now. The containers were out of sight, unless she went down the steep staircase, which was rare.

Paul, the owner of the building that housed their Twins Silver Dream store had been generous and allowed her to break the lease early, considering the circumstances. "Between the loss of your sister and the fact most aren't venturing out anymore, it makes no sense to stay open, Sophie. Come talk after the pandemic ends and maybe we can work something out. You stay safe, now," were Paul's departing words. He was a man of honor.

Thinking back, Sophie questioned herself. *Had she thanked him? Did he know how grateful she felt?* It was a blur to Sophie. She made a mental note to write a thank-you letter to Paul sometime soon.

Tossing her head to release the daydream, Sophie reminded herself aloud, "Go for a walk and listen to the trees."

She dressed for the chill in the air. A hand-knit orange sweater and well-worn, soft scarf around her neck were perfect for this cool autumn morning. She headed past the labyrinth today, smiling as she caught the scent of mint.

The crunch of the leaves and cool air on her face confirmed this was where she ought to be. The thoughts in her mind took her far away from her everyday reality. She murmured, as if Sonya were there with her. "Look at that fallen tree. It looks like a sculpture of a dragon." Bending her neck up at a towering Scotch Pine, "The birds have their own paradise up in the pine trees. So protected and safe." Gazing at the movement of water, "I feel the warmth of the sun on this smooth rock. It's like nature made this chair for me to watch the river flow," she continued, as if still speaking to Sonya.

Sophie rested on the pleasantly warm rock, feeling personally invited into the forest as a special guest. She was grateful for the symphony of birds that provided the musical background. She remained peaceful, contemplative. The water moved gently, carrying an occasional leaf or twig. She sat, relaxed and thoughtful as she watched the river.

Life moves along, demonstrated by the continuous flow of water.

A confession slipped from her lips. "Sonya, I feel you here with me. My life is not moving. With the boutique closed, living alone in the cabin, I can't figure out what I'm supposed to do next. I'm stuck."

As she headed back to her home, Sophie unwound the scarf around her neck. She hadn't realized it was mid-day, and the sun was high in the sky and felt mild. She was admiring the colorful leaves collected on her walk when she saw the big white delivery van pull into her yard.

"Hello, Ma'am, can you please sign here?" said the tall man as he handed her the clipboard with the curled pages. "Just sign, and I'll carry the boxes up to the porch."

The boxes had arrived. She involuntarily dropped the leaves and stood stock still for a moment, unable to lift her arms for the clipboard.

Her mind drifted back to Italy. She was skipping through the narrow streets with Sonya the morning they arrived. "I can't believe we are here, right beside the Ponte Sant' Angelo. This view is enchanting." The sisters had been exploring the colorful facades and secret alleyways before the crowds woke up and ventured out.

Sophie and Sonya's first stop was to a small jewelry studio near the bridge. Aziza and Giovanni were talented artists they met through friends at a gem show a few years ago, before Twins Silver Dream was a reality.

They had been buying each other beautiful, gemstone jewelry since they were teens. "Remember when we bought each other the same ankle bracelet with the rainbow gems dangling from the sterling chain?" recalled Sophie.

"Yes, it was our 17th birthday. It was colorful and had both amethyst and pearl for our birthday month," replied Sonya.

Their love of gemstones and artisan-inspired jewelry gave them the idea of becoming entrepreneurs. "We love jewelry and talking to artists. Maybe we should open a store and share all kinds of beautiful jewelry with others," Sophie declared.

"We could look at gemstones all day and also spend time together! It would be so satisfying!" agreed Sonya.

Twins Silver Dream became a brick-and-mortar boutique, in their hometown a couple of decades later. It turned out the sisters had a brilliant business and marketing sense. Their successful, upscale boutique, with the vast collection of exquisite jewelry, brought smiles to countless customers and friends for years.

The delivery man's voice jarred Sophie back to the present. He was holding the clipboard out to her with a puzzled expression. "Are you okay?"

Sophie suddenly felt very alone and out of sorts. "Yes, where do I sign?" she inquired quietly, reaching out her slightly shaking hand, taking the clipboard.

Later, she brought the large boxes into the living room, past the fireplace, and stacked them next to the bannister. As she glanced up the stairs, her eyes landed on Sonya's portrait painted years before. The hint of a smile and soft, dark curls began to blur as a single tear rolled down Sophie's face. *We loved opening the jewelry. Without you here, I just can't.*

The boxes of jewelry remained unopened. She eventually placed them in the basement, mostly forgotten.

Splish Splash

After the first lunch together, Amanda and Sophie planned frequent visits. "Amanda, let's go explore the woods," Sophie suggested to her friend during their time together. It had been a harsh winter, and they were glad spring was coming in full force. Sophie was truly enjoying the company, after spending most of the last months curled up inside next to the warmth of the fireplace.

"Let's go!" Amanda answered.

Sophie's cabin was her sanctuary. Time spent alone in her thoughts was precious, but sharing time with Amanda was a much-needed reprieve from her solitude.

As they headed towards the forest, Sophie took in a deep, cleansing breath and looked up at the clear blue sky. The azure expanse reminded her of how happy she had become living with acres of forest nearby.

"Don't you love being so close to the trees?" asked Amanda, as she too lifted her face towards the warm sun.

"The trees are my friends and bring me true serenity and joy," answered Sophie.

"I just knew you were a tree hugger," Amanda said delightedly, as they walked quietly towards the welcoming canopy. "The ever-changing forest reminds me that even through struggles the resilience of nature sparks hope and resolve," she declared.

"Yes, we can still grow and dream and meet life at each moment," agreed Sophie. They shared these words of wisdom like two old friends, even though they had met only a year or so ago, on a day that Sophie was feeling overwhelmed and sad. They had become kindred spirits in that short amount of time. Sophie considered Amanda to be her earth angel ever since her friend presented her with the glowing rose quartz on a day she needed it the most.

The babbling brook hummed along the banks and the current was a tad stronger than usual, due to the melting snow just a few weeks earlier. The wild cabbages and cattails peaked above the ground. Crocuses sprouted everywhere, with bright yellow and purple flowers cheerfully decorating their view in every direction. "Spring will be in full bloom before we know it," said Amanda as they admired the delicate flowers.

Earlier, Sophie had shared her labyrinth with Amanda. As they stepped off the porch steps of her cabin, the peonies were full with bright green leaves. They wouldn't bloom for at least another month, but it was wonderful to see the yard beginning to fill out in lush greenery. Amanda smiled and told the story about her long-time neighbor, Al, from years ago. "I had a friend once," she hesitated, as the memory came into view in her mind. It seems like a lifetime ago now," she admitted. "He didn't realize that ants are a big part of how peonies bloom. He thought they were being a nuisance and tried to shake them off of the bushes and was spraying poison on them. I had to rescue the poor ants and explain to him how they nibbled the tight buds and helped open up the flowers!" Sophie loved flowers and, as an avid gardener, she was amused by the story.

As they crossed the side of her home, Amanda said, "Your azaleas look glorious in the sun. The white flowers are really glowing." Dalilah, Amanda's dog, gave the flowers an appreciative sniff.

Sophie smiled and decided then to tell her dear friend how she had felt compelled to build the labyrinth as a remembrance of her sister, Sonya.

"I created the labyrinth during an emotionally challenging time for me, right after I moved into the log cabin. I needed a place to meditate, renew my spirit, and feel grounded," admitted Sophie.

Amanda looked thoughtful and said softly, "Someday, I'll tell you about Willie."

Sophie continued, "I drew up the plans on graph paper, did all the calculations, and figured out how many tons of rocks and other supplies to order. She paused as she gazed at the labyrinth. "Then, I used chalk to plan out the space, measuring and making the circular path just like the picture I imagined, with a rosette in the center," Sophie explained. "I could just imagine Sonya quietly and slowly walking barefoot, towards the center and back again, clearing her mind."

"In the beginning of the project, I thought I could certainly build it by myself. I was wrong," she admitted. "I quickly realized that even though I wasn't rushing, the work was just too strenuous for me to do alone. That's when I contacted the Duck Creek Community College. They suggested a few strong, young students who were happy to earn some extra money," Sophie exclaimed. "They ended up being extremely helpful and dedicated to the task. I was pleased and grateful for the help."

The friends laughed together when she recalled the story of the young college workers asking, "Why do you want to walk in a circle, going nowhere?"

Amanda was intrigued and asked, "Isn't a labyrinth similar to a medicine wheel?"

"Yes! In Native American tradition it's identical," agreed Sophie. "The circular designs have also been found on pottery dating back thousands of years."

Amanda continued, "I remember, years ago, when I taught elementary school I used what we called a finger-labyrinth for students to trace. It was relaxing and calmed their minds. It worked wonders on the children who held extra stress. I've always been fascinated with the concept and wanted to experience a real one."

Amanda and Sophie continued on their stroll through the woods. Once again the two friends had a connection and enjoyed the balance of nature and self-reflection on this beautiful spring afternoon. Sophie had not shared her sanctuary and labyrinth with anyone else. This was developing into an important day.

They were happily hopping from rock to rock, like two children, enjoying the sunshine. It felt natural to stretch and run, with the playfulness the warm spring air encouraged.

"I haven't had this much fun in ages," said Amanda. "I think Dalilah loves it, too." They observed the dog as she ran around exploring. Dalilah wasn't a young dog. In fact, the white around her face and slight limp told a completely different story. The most active she'd been lately was to take their morning walk, and she needed a slight push to cooperate most days.

SPLASH! Sophie slipped on a rock and fell into the water. "Here, let me help...," Amanda started to say as she reached out her hand, also falling, ending up drenched and laughing. Both had on jeans that were now heavy and wet.

"Well, I guess we are on a first name basis with the slippery stones!" said the breathless Sophie. That created another burst of laughter, just like they were school girls at recess.

The sun shone brightly and the warm temperatures reached a new high for the early spring week. When they glanced over, they saw Dalilah comfortably snoozing, nestled in the warm softness of their forgotten sweaters. The sleeping dog was totally unaware of the two women now wet and unintentionally frolicking in the stream. "We aren't exactly mermaids, are we?" chuckled Amanda. Their attempts to stand and gracefully make their way out of the water up to the dry bank was a scene to remember!

Once the two relaxed on a large rock, drying out in the sunshine, they resumed their easy conversation. "I remember a time when Sonya and I were little girls. It must have been in the fall, because the leaves were golden and floating down from the trees. We were running through the yard, on our way to a neighbor's house. I turned around when I realized that Sonya was no longer beside me. She was on the ground, rolling in the grass, cracking up. She could hardly catch her breath from all the laughing. Finally, after a moment to gather herself and recuperate, Sonya burst out, *I tripped over a leaf!*

"We talked about that day so many times. It became a joke. Every time one of us fell, no matter where we were, we would say together, *Must have tripped over a leaf.* "I guess you had to be there," recalled Sophie with a wide grin.

Amanda laughed, "You two sound so adorable as little girls."

It felt good to feel young, carefree, and sitting next to a dear friend in the sunshine. It was also a new experience to recall memories without the tears. So many good times.

Cleansing away the cobwebs of winter, spending time in the labyrinth, and amongst the trees was meditative. "We should spend time in the woods more often," said Amanda, mimicking Sophie's thoughts. "A swing would be perfect over there under the trees where Daliliah is sleeping," suggested Amanda.

"I've thought about a swing. My bank account is dwindling, so right now there aren't going to be new purchases," Sophie confessed. "It is a great idea, though."

They sat together comfortably, each caught up in their own thoughts. Amanda was concocting new recipes for goat's milk soap in her creative mind. Sophie was wondering what sort of jobs might be available in town to earn extra money. Both women were lost in thought, comfortable in the silence, surrounded by the wisdom of old trees.

Ruthie Louise

Amanda awoke to a gentle rain and birds singing outside her bedroom window.

It was barely dawn when her husband, Tony, handed her a steaming cup of her favorite coffee. She stretched, smiled with joy, and fluffed her pillow. She loved the light blue Italian silk pillowcase that Sophie had given her as a gift. "Your long hair will be softer and less tangled when you sleep on silk," her friend promised.

She was sipping the hot coffee with no intention of getting out of bed just yet. Her new kitten, Willow, was curled up beside her. The adorable gray, fluff ball was a rescue from Small Wonders, described in the pamphlet as the *pet recovery sanctuary. How could anyone visit Small Wonders without deciding on a new pet?* wondered Amanda.

She was content listening to the rain and the music of nature. Rainy mornings without big plans were at the top of her favorite things list. As the birds sang sweetly, she thought, *I haven't painted in quite some time. I wonder where the old easel is?* recalling her very first painting of the pretty little bluebird. Once the inspiration struck, she really enjoyed the relaxation of painting.

Amanda was remembering something else from years gone by. Her fireplace mantle in her cottage when she resided in town was covered in mementos. There was a special black feather, several crystals, driftwood, and other items on what she called her Willie altar.

What a lonely time. *On some days I felt isolated and withdrawn during the coronavirus quarantine. Thanks to the blessings of a tree, other days often felt exquisite. I have my dear, forty-foot tall oak friend to thank. The tree, who I named Willie, allowed me to settle at his trunk and be transported to a more harmonious time. The serene adventures left me feeling calm and happy. I sometimes found tokens of our times together nearby afterwards. I love holding these treasures,* Amanda remembered fondly.

I'm going to tell Sophie about Willie soon, she decided.

Now, living on the farm suited her. She

laughed when she recalled telling Sophie, "I read an article online where people pay money to do yoga with baby goats! Can you imagine Tony trying to herd our newest babies to the field, with a group of young people exercising in upscale yoga gear?" Her mind drifted back to her painting, *Maybe I could capture that fiasco on canvas.*

Amanda nuzzled cozily beneath her covers daydreaming when her husband's deep voice startled her. "Remember, I'll be gone all day fishing," Tony reminded Amanda. "The morning rain will make the bass roam up to the top of the creek, so I'd better get moving. I have a feeling we will be grilling fish tonight for dinner," exclaimed her husband. "By the way, thanks for making me the sandwiches," he said with a wink.

Amanda stretched and remembered she was due at Sophie's later that morning.

"Hello, are you awake, Sophie?" Amanda called from the front porch of the log cabin. As with many visits, Amanda arrived with something scrumptious. "I baked cinnamon rolls, just out of the oven," Amanda said. "I hope you're hungry!" she called, holding the pottery covered with a linen cloth.

"Please come in. I've been up for awhile. I'm so glad the rain has stopped. Grab a mug and help yourself to coffee," Sophie said easily. The routine was becoming automatic. Sophie added another log to the fire as the two friends sat and ate in comfortable tranquility. It seemed the silence was as valuable as the many times they had sat in extended conversation. The friendship was effortless.

"So, what did the letter from your old landlord, Paul, say?" Amanda inquired after both had finished their breakfast. Sophie often walked with Amanda down the long driveway to retrieve her mail when she was heading home. The letter from Paul had arrived a few days before.

Sophie had opened the letter with apprehension. She knew Paul was generous, yet he also lost a significant amount of money when he allowed her to simply walk away from the lease for Twins Silver Dream, the boutique Sonya and Sophie had run on Main Street. Sonya's death had crippled Sophie. She had finally written Paul a letter of gratitude over a year later. It was a carefully crafted, old-fashioned letter. Although long overdue, sending that letter felt wonderful.

Sophie handed the white envelope to Amanda, watching her open and read the response Paul had sent.

Dearest Sophie,

You've been on my mind. Thanks for the kind words. It was my pleasure to lend a helping hand during the time of Sonya's death. The resi-

dents of Duck Creek Township have shown their resilience and ability to rally together. Please let me know if you have an interest in resurrecting Twins Silver Dream. The property remains available, including all the shelving and lights we installed to display your jewelry. Bryan has inquired about the space to add a brick oven area to the cafe for his new pizza idea. I told him I'd let him know after I spoke to you.

By the way, a few days after I received your letter, I was visited by a woman looking for you. She mentioned she'd been trying to find out where you'd moved. Rather than give your new address, I hope you don't mind that I shared your phone number. She was vague, a little secretive. She said it was a personal matter. I didn't recognize her from town, and you know how we pretty much know everyone here, right? Her name is Ruthie Louise.

> *Best Regards,*
> *Paul*
> *S&P Property Management, LLC*

"Wow, Sophie, are you going to consider opening your boutique again?" inquired Amanda. "And by the way, did I ever tell you the turquoise ring that Tony bought for me the first Christmas we were together came from your place? I kept the pretty organza bag with silver stars on it and found the business card after you and I met.

It took me a while to realize it was your boutique. You were directly next to Bryan's Cafe. Am I right?"

"Yes, as a matter of fact, we probably ate enough of Bryan's shrimp salad to keep him in business while we were neighbors," Sophie confessed. "While Sonya and I were away on the buying trip to Italy, I think Devin and Lily, our two employees, stopped by Bryan's almost daily for lattes," Sophie added.

"The boutique decision will have to wait. Today, my mind is on the visitor who is arriving later today, actually in about thirty minutes. That lady, Ruthie Louise, is coming. Her phone call came the same day I received Paul's note. She didn't share details of what she wanted, and it sounded mysterious," Sophie explained.

"Oh, I didn't know you were having company. Let me get out of here," Amanda said in a rushed voice.

"Well, to be honest, Amanda. I was hoping you'd stay. I'm not sure what this woman has to say. It feels like it's important, and I'm not sure I want to be alone."

"Of course. Yes, I'll hang out if you want. Tony is fishing again, and my house is empty. What if I sit in the kitchen and, when you answer the door, you can sit in the living room with her? I'll be in the next room if you need me," Amanda said as she moved through the kitchen door.

Settled in with a last-minute plan of support, both women stiffened a bit when the knock rang through the cabin. As promised, Amanda remained in the kitchen, quietly waiting.

Sophie opened the door to find a middle-aged, blonde woman. Tall and muscular, she looked like an athlete. Sophie, not a small woman, looked up at the stranger, greeting her with a nod as she gestured for her to enter.

"Thank you for allowing me to come to see you in person. I realize this all seems so peculiar and secretive. It's that what I want to share with you is so incredibly personal," Ruthie Louise spoke in a hushed tone.

Amanda listened to the murmur of voices from the living room, but couldn't catch the gist of the conversation. It sounded cordial, so she wasn't worried.

"Well, is there something I can do for you?" Sophie inquired.

"No, thank you. This will be a short visit. I'm here to express my heartfelt gratitude," said Ruthie Louise, as she placed her hand on her chest gently.

The two women sat side by side on the sofa.

Sophie leaned in to hear what Ruthie Louise had to say, who had a serious look on her face.

Ruthie Louise took a deep breath. She looked directly into Sophie's eyes, keeping her hand over her heart. Sophie got the impression she had rehearsed what she was about to reveal. "I was driving home from visiting my nephew last year, just past the Duck Creek exit. Out of nowhere, a tractor trailer swerved into my lane. I don't remember much of what happened afterwards, other than the sound of sirens. The closest hospital was Sacred Heart, which is where I was transported," she explained in a quiet voice.

"It's because of your sister, Sonya, that I'm alive today," Ruthie Louise announced.

"The paperwork that I was given after the long stay in the hospital named Sonya as the donor. The accident severely damaged my heart. My body eventually accepted the new heart. Through complicated surgical procedures, and a long touch and go recuperation, I'm able to live a healthy and comfortable lifestyle," Ruthie Louise shared.

"I have you to thank. It's taken me quite a while to find you. I know how hard it must've been to lose your sister to COVID. I'm sure you'll agree, this is not news that should be shared over the phone. I thank you for allowing me to come to your home. I'm so grateful for your sister," Ruthie Louise finished, still holding her hand on her heart.

Sophie sat perfectly still. Stunned. Translucent tears flowed unchecked down her brown cheeks. She had known Sonya was an organ donor; they both were. It was documented on their drivers' licenses. She was told that day at Sacred Heart that Sonya's lungs were destroyed because of the virus. There was a brief discussion that other organs were considered healthy. Perhaps she was told about the donation? It was all a total blur.

Ah, Sonya, part of you is keeping this woman alive. Unbelievable, she thought without speaking.

Still looking into one another's eyes, Ruthie Louise took Sophie's hand and lifted it to her heart. There was complete silence, other than the rhythmic beat Sophie could feel and hear with her palm. "Sonya," was all Sophie could whisper.

Amanda sat in the kitchen with curiosity. The talking had stopped, yet she did not hear the door open or close. *Are they still in the living room? Does Sophie need my support in some way?* Amanda asked herself.

She peeked through the kitchen door, tentatively, to see the two women sitting in silence. Tears streaming down both faces. Confused, but certain there was no danger involved, Amanda entered the room quietly and sat over in a corner chair, attempting to be invisible.

Ruthie Louise and Sophie embraced. It was a long and intimate encounter. Amanda observed, knowing there was something special happening. Thankfully, neither of the women looked in Amanda's direction over in the corner of the room by the kitchen door.

Amanda could feel the intensity of the hug from across the room. Although she was not informed about the situation, it was obvious there was an enormous connection.

Ruthie Louise handed Amanda an envelope as she departed, "My contact information is enclosed, in case you'd like to keep in touch." She walked briskly towards the front door, knowing she accomplished her mission. Ruthie Louise allowed the tears to flow freely on her face as she exited Sophie's home.

When the door closed, Amanda let out a loud sigh. Sophie jumped. "Dear me,

I didn't know you were in the room. Did you hear the whole conversation?"

"No, I came in while you two were hugging," Amanda said. "It looked like you were two long-lost friends."

"Amanda, part of Sonya is still alive!" she excitedly told her friend.

"What do you mean? Amanda replied. Sophie replayed the whole conversation, explaining about the organ donation and how perfect the timing happened to be for Ruthie Louise.

Sophie described, "I truly don't remember much about that day. I was in shock."

"What's in your hand?" Amanda asked.

"She gave me her contact information in case we want to stay in touch," Sophie said, distracted.

Knowing Sophie needed some time to process this news, Amanda gave her friend a quick hug. "I'm going to head home," she said quietly. "This is such amazing news. Let me know if you want to talk later, okay?" she volunteered as she left.

"I'm glad you were here. Talk to you later," said Sophie as Amanda closed the door.

Chocolate Wisdom

Sophie walked amongst the trees by moonlight. She hadn't slept soundly for over a week, after the emotional events of meeting Ruthie Louise. *I think best when I'm in the forest. I should have come here right away,* thought Sophie.

The night was cold, but clear, with a bright moon and so many stars. One star in particular was shining extra brightly. She smiled as she thought, *Hello, sweet sister.*

Sophie dressed warmly with her old, sapphire blue coat buttoned up, and a fuzzy alpaca scarf haphazardly wrapped around her neck. Her hair was getting longer, and her black braids hung down her back, underneath the warm hat she'd grabbed at the last minute. The scuffed brown leather boots had seen lots of walking, since they'd been her favorites for nearly a decade. They slipped on easily, and her flannel pajama bottoms tucked inside the tall boots without effort.

"I think Amanda had a good idea," she said to her tree-friends as she passed by the stream. "A swing would be perfect right here. Maybe someday." She paused and sat down carefully on one of the big rocks. Her mind wandered to a day when the pleasant sun greeted spring. She was amused as she recollected the afternoon she had introduced Amanda to the wonders of her forest. They ended up soaked and drying out on this very same rock. It was the early days of a cherished friendship.

She walked on, knowing her property well, even in the dark. Crickets were chirping, keeping her company. She listened to the branches and dried leaves crunching under her feet. The moon seemed to follow and watch over her, which she found comforting.

"Sonya, your heart lives on inside a woman named Ruthie Louise," Sophie murmured to herself. "I felt it. I felt your heart beating," she whispered, almost like a prayer.

Taking a deep breath, and watching the puff of vapor as she exhaled, Sophie kept walking and circled back toward her cabin. Unaware of how long she'd been silently thinking and slowly ambling surrounded by nature, she could hear what she assumed was a great horned owl high in the tree-top. She glanced up, but couldn't see him. It was reassuring to know the gentle night-time creature shared her space. Time spent in the woods seemed to nourish her soul and settle her mind. *Right now my brain is zig-zagging in a million different directions, but in a strange way I feel more centered out here,* she admitted to herself.

As she followed the stream, it's icy edges gleamed in the moonlight. She could hear the frozen ice making soft crackling sounds, reminding her of life's never-ending transformation. Even in winter, mother nature hibernates and slows down, but readies herself for spring.

Her hands were chilly, and she automatically put them into the deep pockets of her coat, which once belonged to Sonya. Her left hand wrapped around a forgotten smooth rock, leftover from last winter. She remembered with love, *Sonya was always picking up treasures: rocks in the woods, shells on the beach, and feathers under the trees. She used to say they were lucky treasures.*

As she went inside her cabin, Sophie felt the welcoming warmth of her sanctuary. She had left a few lights on, along with the golden salt-lamp in the corner. The subtle shadows the lights created offered a familiar and soothing atmosphere. She peeled off the boots, happy that her feet were warm with soft socks she usually wore to bed on cold nights. She then took off her hat and scarf, and as she was about to drape the coat on a chair, she remembered the stone. When she reached into the pocket, she took the rock and a few other things and laid them on the table, next to her fragrant bowl of pinecones.

It was still night, and her bed felt like it was waiting for her. *Ah, home sweet home,* went through her mind, as the cuckoo clock chimed twice. Ginger, her fluffy orange tabby, was already snuggled at the bottom of her bed and purred when she disturbed her slumber. Sophie sunk freely into the comforter and slept without dreams until the sun came up.

The next morning, Sophie slept in, but instead of feeling groggy like sometimes when she stayed in bed late, she felt refreshed. She awoke hungry and immediately thought of making pumpkin pancakes. *Funny, no wonder my jeans have been snug. I'm thinking about my next meal as soon as I wake up,* she snickered as she rolled out of bed. She had noticed that her already generous backside was expanding. *Thank heavens for elastic waistbands and flowing skirts.*

She knew she was meeting Amanda for an afternoon in town, but had plenty of time for a big breakfast and shower. Sophie sauntered into the kitchen wearing her comfortable, thick robe and fuzzy slippers. "First, coffee," she said as she pulled out a tall, rounded orange and yellow pottery mug. She added a sprinkle of nutmeg and almond milk. She enjoyed the Sumatra aroma wafting through the kitchen.

Sophie put on some lively Motown music. She swayed to the music. The song was by a really old favorite group, The Temptations. She sang along, "You are sunshine on a rainy day."

The deep, nutty flavor of the Sumatra coffee satisfied Sophie, and she could tell already that it was going to be a wonderful day.

As she stood at the stove, the bacon sizzled and she finished flipping the pancakes, adding a few chocolate morsels.

It was a sure bet that the two friends would be stopping at Sage and Thyme, the little store Amanda loved. Amanda was planning another batch of goat's milk soap, and that always required supplies from the quaint store owned by Tommy and Leya. Sage and Thyme was a treasure trove of healthy living products and unique little gifts. They also owned a lavender farm, which Sophie frequented in spring.

She began making a mental list of the essential oils she needed for her collection. *Eucalyptus, in case I get a winter cold; lavender to add to my bath; and, perhaps, something citrusy to remind me that warmer months are just ahead. Actually, many months ahead. I hope we visit The Novel Book Shoppe. The small book store used to have such lively book club discussions. It was entertaining,* remembered Sophie.

After her second cup of coffee and her decadent breakfast, she knew it was time to shower and get ready for her outing. *This little slice of heaven,* referring to her pumpkin pancakes, *will surely last me all day. I'm so full!*

Before showering, Sophie picked out a long skirt with shades of a swirled blue design and a few sequins. It was a heavy cotton, perfect with a soft white, loose-fitting cable knit sweater. She rummaged through her sock drawer to locate the tall boot socks, which just happened to be decorated with polka dots in a rainbow of colors. "So festive," she said to herself smiling.

Sophie had a small amount of Amanda's homemade body wash left in the old fashioned glass container in the shower. It made her skin feel so soft. During the winter months, especially, her skin was dry, and the luxurious wash felt wonderful. *Maybe Amanda's new recipe for goat soap will be moisturizing, too,* she hoped.

After she dressed, Sophie looked in her jewelry box, which was really the entire top drawer of her dresser. *You can never have too much jewelry,* she smiled as she thought of one of the many mantras she and Sonya shared. Her collection was not exactly organized and neat, so she mentally added that to her to-do list. Sophie picked a large, sparkling rainbow topaz topped with an oval blue quartz to go with the blue skirt. She added a few sterling bangle bracelets and chandelier earrings. *Perhaps I'm going a tad overboard with the accessories today.* She was feeling wonderful.

Sophie slipped into her favorite brown leather boots, reminding her of the long nighttime walk that left her feeling relaxed. *The trees really make me feel better. I should spend more time outdoors.* Nearly ready to leave, she remembered, *Oh, I almost forgot the lucky stone in my pocket from last night. Where did I leave it?* she asked herself. The long coat was still draped on the chair, next to the table. In a small pile sat the contents of her pocket. *Let's see, I have a smooth river stone, a few pine needles and…a Dove chocolate!* The sweet little treat had the foil wrapper, still looking new. *Well, I have to open this and see what words of wisdom await me,* she said with glee. *Yogi tea and Dove chocolate never disappoint.* Inside the wrinkled wrapper a message in gold foil spoke to her: *Because you can.*

Alarming Announcement

Amanda and Sophie arrived within minutes of one another at Sage and Thyme. The tinkle of the welcoming bell rang as they each walked inside. The ladies embraced. "Hi Sophie," Amanda said with a smile. "Isn't it a lovely day for shopping? Doesn't it smell amazing in here?"

Sophie replied, "Yes, the blended scents are incredible. I have a feeling it's going to be a rewarding shopping day."

Taking a long whiff, Sophie smiled and located the lavender essential oil she used in her nighttime bath rituals. Amanda moved towards the display of local honey, which she planned to incorporate into her newest goat's milk creations.

The store was mostly empty and quiet. Amanda paused. On the wall right next to the honey display was a large painting by a local artist. Sophie glanced over as Amanda gazed at the majestic tree in the painting. The tree had a magical look. She overheard her friend whisper, "Willie, this reminds me of you," as if it were a friend.

Just then Leya approached to greet the ladies, "How nice to see the two of you today. It's always a pleasure to greet my favorite customers." Leya's cat, the calico known to hang out at the shoppe, breezed by to find her cushion by the counter as they spoke. "I've switched the displays around a bit, consolidating the products as we get closer to the closing date," Leya explained.

"Did you say closing?" inquired Sophie.

"What's closing?" Amanda interrupted as she overheard their conversation from down the aisle.

"So sorry." said Leya. "You don't know about the new shopping center coming in the spring? It's not totally official, but the large plot of land is being purchased down by Duck Creek and the company is planning a shopping center. Our small businesses here in town are mostly closing or trying to figure out how to possibly compete. It's been in the paper. You haven't seen it?" asked Leya.

"Wait!" said Amanda coming closer, trying to

catch up with the news. "A shopping center is being built close to Duck Creek, down by my farm?"

"Yes, out there someplace. I'm not sure of the exact location, but right outside of town," explained Leya.

"Wow, that forest area near us has been a natural habitat for so many animals. I always assumed it was an environmentally protected area. We need to investigate," declared Sophie.

The shop owner suggested, "If you go down to city hall, the whole map and projected building is on a poster displayed in the lobby."

"Thanks, Leya, we will definitely look this over," Sophie ended the conversation by moving towards the cash register, her basket filled with bath items, essential oils, as well as some spices for cooking. She bent down to pet the kitty, as Amanda paid for her purchases. Sophie remembered they called him Chester as she gave her a welcome scratch behind his ears. The friendly cat responded with a purr of gratitude.

Waving a quick goodbye, the two friends made a beeline down to City Hall. They walked by the hair salon called Citrine, which had been on this end of town ever since they could remember. They waved a hasty hello to a few friends entering the salon, but didn't stop. Their mission to get to city hall hurried them along.

Both Sophie and Amanda felt deep dismay at the possibility of a shopping mall anywhere close to their homes. *What about the forest and animals?* they thought independently.

The friends were quiet as they turned the corner. With the wind blowing, Amanda had to rewrap her scarf around her neck and tuck her head down against the cold. Walking into the old building, they noticed it had not changed and still looked quite impressive. The polished floors and old wood gleamed. The foyer's tall ceilings gave an air of days gone by as the wrought-iron chandeliers hung stately overhead. Pretty patterns of light danced along the walls and ceiling. A large easel in the center of the room held a detailed map showing the proposed construction. It looked very official, with a logo on the bottom reading: Smith & Sons Property Development. Beneath it in finer print showed an address in the city and phone number.

They stood alone, examining the plans, with graph lines and tiny print. Sophie suddenly exclaimed, "This long building must be a strip mall, and it's right next to your farm, Amanda!"

Amanda moaned and replied, "Look! This large parking lot, with endless asphalt, is really close to your cabin. This whole map is in between our homes."

Their hands grasped one another's as they both shook their heads and said "No!" simultaneously. As they turned to leave, Sophie grabbed a business card and stuffed it into her coat pocket.

"This cannot happen," choked Sophie. Amanda shook her head in complete agreement.

"It's so cold," stammered Amanda. "Let's go to Bryan's Cafe and get a cup of coffee and talk more."

"Okay. Maybe Bryan knows details. I can't understand how this all started without us knowing anything?" replied Sophie.

The brilliant mid-morning sun glared down, but added no warmth as they walked to the next street, shivering. Finally, they came to the café.

"Welcome, it's been way too long," said Bryan cheerily as they started taking off their coats. "Here, have a seat over by the corner, away from the door." They had a warm, but graceless hug, clumsily bumping into each other. The three briefly laughed together, as only long-time friends can.

Sophie jumped right in, "Tell us everything you know about this threatening shopping mall. We just left city hall, and the plans look like the construction is right next to Duck's Creek. Right between our properties."

"It all started about a month or two ago, when old man Higgins passed away. He owned all that land. His only child, Jacob Higgins, who lives in Riverside, probably decided he no longer wanted to be bothered with the taxes from being a land-owner. We are guessing he just wants the money. Some big company offered him a good sum, and he jumped on it. I don't believe it's a done deal. They haven't even gone to settlement yet," explained Bryan. "The business owners in town are devastated, and some have already talked about closing down. There's talk about a Super Walmart, and one of those huge gas stations with fast food, called Sheetz," Bryan elaborated.

"Here, have a seat. Would you like something warm? Tea? Coffee?" questioned Bryan. "I'll send Casey over in a minute. Let me finish up in the back, and I'll take a break and join you."

Sophie and Amanda settled in at their table, even more disturbed, now that Bryan confirmed the news. The place was bustling for a mid-week afternoon. Almost every table was filled with happy, talkative customers. It was one of the most popular restaurants in town, no doubt because Bryan made everyone feel welcome and the food was delicious. Many of the menu items were made with local produce. Amanda supplied Bryan with fresh herbs and vegetables from their farm, along with goat cheese that Tony made.

Casey stopped by with their favorite warm beverages, knowing the women so well. They sipped their chai tea and freshly brewed coffee, enjoying the warmth.

"I had no idea that John Higgins died. Did you?" asked Sophie.

"No, I only met him one time, back when he and his wife sold eggs and vegetables down at the Farmer's Market, years ago. After she died, he moved away, and I haven't heard anything about him since. That's been a few years though," explained Amanda.

"I remember his son, Jacob, was an only child. He's about my age, if I recall. He went to Blue Creek High with Sonya and me. He was on the basketball team," Sophie remarked.

Sophie was absorbed in thought when she heard Amanda ask, "Do you think the farmhouse is still on the land? It was close to the stream, wasn't it? Maybe we should take a long walk and check it out later today," suggested Amanda.

After stopping at a few tables to say hi to other customers, Bryan made his way over to them. He sat down with a heavy umph. "I apologize. I assumed you knew," he said with a touch of sadness. "The plans were drawn up so quickly because they were originally meant for a plot of land down in Berkley, but the zoning couldn't be worked out.

Only a few changes were needed to fit the Higgin's farmland. The attorneys discovered the farm is already zoned for business. Surprisingly, the law firm found out all the property along there is zoned for business, including your land, too, I suppose."

"Wait until Tony finds out about this fiasco! He will be so upset," said Amanda, nearly in tears. "Our farm is quiet. Knowing Sophie is our closest neighbor is really a comfort. I always hoped that property would stay as is, due to Duck Creek running through the land. I thought it was environmentally or historically protected in some way."

"I don't think I could bear all the obnoxious noise. Plus, those glaring parking lot lights and cars will disturb the peace. I can't believe this is happening," Sophie slumped her head onto her hand with a heavy sigh.

"We have planned a town meeting at city hall next Saturday afternoon at 2:00 p.m. Jacob Higgins lives not too far away, in Riverside, so he will be here. He says he will answer all our questions. Jacob will stay around until the papers are signed and the sale is official. Can you both join the meeting?" Bryan asked.

"Of course, I'll start making a list of questions. Will the representatives from Smith & Sons Property Development also be there?" questioned Sophie.

"That's a very good question, but I don't know the answer. Both the owners and the foreman of the construction crew have been invited, but the Smith Company has not responded," Bryan replied.

"Small businesses are getting a raw deal all over. The government loans during the pandemic were a joke," chimed in Amanda. "We have many unpretentious, family-owned shops in our little town. The ones that survived the battering of the coronavirus now have to fight against big corporations with zero empathy. It's very frustrating."

The bright afternoon sun was high and felt comforting on their faces as they left the safety of the cafe. "My long skirt is keeping me warm, but this wind is blowing it all over," said Sophie, as she wrestled with her skirt whipping around her boots. Annoying and amusing at the same time, she couldn't help but let out a little grunt of irritation. "Do you have time to come back to my place and start drafting a list of questions with me?" she asked Amanda.

"Yes, I'll meet you at the cabin in a few minutes. I'm going to try to reach Tony first, but when he's fishing, he usually doesn't bother with looking at his phone," stated Amanda.

Amanda stopped by the farmhouse, just on the off chance that Tony had come home early. No luck. Amanda was anxious to share the news, hoping he would have some solutions. Dalilah Belle, her old dog, jumped around as if she'd been gone for days. "Dalilah Belle, why don't you come with me to Sophie's?" Amanda cooed to her beloved friend.

Sophie parked her little blue car and walked with purpose towards her porch, still fuming about the whole Walmart situation. Before going inside, she gathered as many logs from the wood pile as she could manage, thinking a fire would soothe her.

Settled in front of a blazing fire, the two friends put their heads together, ready to do battle. "I'll make us some tea," said Amanda, completely at ease in her friend's home. Ginger, Sophie's usually shy cat, curled up next to the hearth without a care in the world, unaware of the tension in the room. She purred softly and licked her paws. Sensing the turmoil, an agitated Dalilah followed Amanda to the kitchen.

"I'm not sure what questions to ask," said a defeated looking Sophie. "Do we have any rights, just living next to the land?" They sipped their tea in silence, but got nowhere with the questions. In one afternoon, their lives were turned upside down with no solutions in sight.

"I'm just overwhelmed and sad," admitted Amanda.

"Do you feel like hiking over to Higgins Farm?" Sophie asked. "We certainly aren't making any headway here."

"Sure," Amanda sighed.

Sophie ran up the stairs and put on a pair of heavy jeans to keep her warm. She tossed the skirt on her bed.

Both women bundled up, pulling on gloves Sophie kept in a basket in her hall closet. They knew it would be a long trek into the woods.

Amanda pulled out her favorite multi-colored hand knit hat with funky earflaps. "Did I ever tell you about wearing this hat when I first met Tony? It was towards the end of the pandemic, and I went shopping at the market. I had my cart loaded up with Ben & Jerry's ice cream, even more than usual," she chuckled. "It seems like a long time ago. I recall bumping into him accidentally, looking up and seeing his dark, smiling face. His amused eyes were happy and he said something like, 'Nice hat.' I thought for a second he was poking fun at me. Then I noticed he was wearing a cowboy hat. I believe in serendipity," Amanda stated as they headed out the door with Dalilah Belle following along closely.

Sophie just nodded with a genuine affection at her friend. Yes, she knew the tale well, but also realized it was one of Amanda's favorite stories.

The sky had turned gray, and before they had gotten very far, snowflakes fell gently along the path ahead of them. They started walking towards Amanda's farm, but turned down the long, winding driveway toward the old Higgin's place, instead. The rusted mailbox leaned a little to the left, a remnant from an accident years ago. "It's a good thing we aren't driving. I don't think a car could even make it through with all the overgrowth. I can't even see the driveway," declared Sophie.

"It doesn't look like anybody has been back here in ages," Amanda concurred.

The women fought with heavy branches and fallen trees. The pine trees swayed in the wind, while they traipsed along broken bits of a driveway that had seen better days, now covered in branches, old leaves, and pine needles. The brambles stuck to Dalilah who had regained her energy from the nap by the fire and now ran in circles around Amanda and Sophie. The two friends walked and walked, almost certain they were going towards the center of the property. The canopy of red maple and sweet gum trees were a blaze of red and gold just a few months ago, but now loomed barren overhead, awaiting the beauty of spring.

A row of stately, still-green cypress trees peeked through up ahead. "I think those trees will lead us to the farmhouse," suggested Amanda. The snow hurried down heavier now, but the friends weren't cold. The long hike had warmed them.

"Look up. The trees are magical." Sophie observed, smiling for the first time since they had been at the cafe in town. Amanda and Sophie stopped for a few minutes and enjoyed the snow glistening at dusk.

"I always feel like trees remind me to slow down and take it easy. Walking here, I feel more relaxed," Amanda added. The forest nurtured their spirits and the beautiful snow added to the serenity. "That Smith Development can't chop down all these amazing trees!" cried Amanda.

Her hands curling in response, Sophie's anger welled up within her as Amanda cried out, both women in sync with the forest and each other. Sophie reached her arm out towards Amanda. Amanda found her hand as the women grasped each other for a brief moment of solidarity.

They could see a crumbling red brick, two-story house up ahead, with wide stone steps leading up to a generous wrap-around porch. Once sturdy, the faded white railing split in pieces along the sagging wooden floor boards. The home had seen better days. "Look at that stained glass window above the door," Sophie said excitedly.

"I wonder what the inside looks like?"

Amanda said with a curious tone. "The windows are all boarded up, and probably have been since Higgins left all those years ago. I guess his son has not been here at all," whispered Amanda mournfully.

"Did the son, Jacob, even come see his old house before deciding to sell?" commented Sophie.

The snow blanketed the property now. The women looked around for a few minutes and made the trek back to their respective homes, leaving saddened footprints behind them.

Gone Fishing

"Honey, I'm home," called Tony as he opened the front door of the farmhouse.

He was dressed in big, dirty work boots, overalls, and a flannel shirt topped with an old, heavy canvas coat. Amanda sat in the rocker, lost in her deep thoughts, hoping the events of the last day were a bad dream. Tony noticed her bleak expression as soon as he walked into the room. He went over and gave her a kiss on the cheek and said, "You look upset."

"Come, sit down. I have news to share, and you are not going to like it," Amanda blurted out. He tugged off his coat, threw it across the couch, and sat down in the other rocker by the fireplace.

"I already know. I saw Daniel from the hardware store out by the creek," Tony said with a huff.

"I was wishing it wasn't true, but guessing by your face, it is. The Higgin's land is really being sold?"

"Yes," she added, "but there's a meeting in town on Saturday, and the whole community will be gathered to protest," she continued hopefully.

Tony didn't look convinced that anything could be done. Anger creased his forehead. "Why would anybody listen to us?" he challenged.

"Take off those filthy boots and show me your catch," Amanda said with a slight grin, trying to steer the conversation. Tony had high blood pressure, and she didn't want him to get upset over something they could do nothing to change.

"Well, I told you we would be grilling fish, and I was right. Come, take a look at these beauties!" he stated proudly. "Rainbow trout big enough for dinner and a few perch we can freeze for another time."

"Let's fry the fish tonight. It's too cold and snowy outside to light the grill. I think I'll make macaroni and cheese. I need some comfort food," admitted Amanda.

That night, they snuggled in bed, contemplating all the destruction and changes that would occur in Duck Creek. "I wish we could wake up from this nightmare," whispered Amanda.

Tony and Amanda reminisced about expanding the garden, preparing a yard for the baby goats, and adding the chicken coop last spring. "Our farm is just the way we always dreamed it would be," said Tony.

"I really love our chicken coop, Tony. It's extra special because you built it. Even though you laughed at me when I showed you pictures, you made it just the way I wanted. It looks like a miniature version of our farmhouse. I smile every time I walk by. You don't know how much I appreciate your talents, my dear, " Amanda said sleepily.

Even though the land sale sounded inevitable at this point, they promised each other they would attend the meeting. "Maybe the attorneys will discover some loophole with the zoning that will prevent the strip mall," Tony asserted. He wrapped Amanda in a tight hug as their breathing synchronized.

Pearls and Blue Topaz

Sophie had been thinking about Jacob Higgins for two straight days. Finally, she got up the nerve to look him up. "If I'm going to save our little town, I've got to be proactive," she gave herself a pep talk. Eventually, Sophie found his information online and discovered Riverside was fairly close.

She recalled, so clearly, the purchase he had made at Twins Silver Dream when they had first opened. He described the gift he was seeking as, "Something special for a lady friend. I'm trying to impress her."

In high school, Jacob had been a popular athlete on the basketball team. Years later, standing at the jewelry counter, he appeared to be slightly shy and even humble. Sophie remembered thinking she liked the humble Jacob much better than the ego-driven high-schooler she remembered.

Sophie and Sonya had helped him select a beautiful pendant and earring set. The pearls were surrounded by light blue topaz. "The blue topaz will enhance communication," Sonya explained to Jacob. "And pearls are a perfect symbol of integrity and honesty."

"That sounds exactly what I was hoping for," Jacob exclaimed. Sophie recalled he had requested the prettiest box and gift wrapping. The twins wondered how his lady-friend liked the gift, but Jacob hadn't come back to the shop after that one time.

Sophie sat at the kitchen table, staring at his phone number for at least twenty minutes. Taking a deep breath, she tapped his number on her cell phone. Her heart pounded. Without giving much thought to what she was going to say, she listened to the phone ring with anticipation.

"Hello," she heard Jacob's deep voice.

"Um, hi. Is this Jacob Higgins?" Sophie's voice sounded strong and confident, despite her rapid heartbeat and sweaty palms.

"Yes, who's calling?" he inquired.

"Jacob, this is Sophie Walker, from Duck Creek."

"Sophie, the jewelry aficionado?" he asked with a friendly voice.

"Ha, yes! I'm surprised you remember me," she confessed.

"Well, you and your sister gave me wonderful advice about the jewelry purchase that one time. Your sister suggested the set I bought would facilitate integrity, if I remember correctly. Unfortunately, there was strong communication and honesty."

"Oh, I'm glad to hear that. Wait, why do you say unfortunately, though?" Sophie asked.

"My lady friend loved the gift. She wore it often and also kept it when she dumped me. She was very honest. Apparently, she liked the gift more than she liked me," Jacob explained with a hint of disappointment.

Sophie paused, trying to think what she could say to lighten up the conversation.

"Wow, that's not exactly what I was expecting," she stammered a bit before he interrupted.

"That was quite a while ago, not to worry," Jacob laughed.

"What makes you get in touch, Sophie?"

"I was talking to Bryan, over at the cafe. He

mentioned you'd be in town sometime soon. I just thought we could get together, maybe for a cup of coffee or something?"

"I'd like that, Sophie. What time do you close your Twins Silver Dream shop? Could we meet for dinner? I'll be in town on Friday. How does that work for you?"

"Yes, Friday would be lovely," not mentioning the fact the shop was no longer open. "Let's plan for seven o'clock," she answered, thinking their conversation was going way better than she expected.

"Do you still live in the brownstone on Main?" Jacob questioned.

"No, I'm out in the woods these days," she laughed. "I live in a log cabin now. I'll text my address to you on Friday. How about if I throw some dinner together so we don't have to drive into town?" she offered.

"That's generous of you, Sophie. It will be nice to catch up. I'll see you on Friday," Jacob said before he hung up.

Sophie sat at the kitchen table, stunned by how easy the conversation had been.

That wasn't complicated or even awkward at all, she mused. *Now, to convince Jacob the strip mall deal is a bad idea.*

Bubbles

Long, soaking baths were a luxury that Sophie indulged in quite frequently, especially when it was cold outside. *I can't wait to use my new lavender essential oil and soap from Sage and Thyme,* she thought. Sophie brought in her favorite yellow flannel pajamas and fuzzy robe and hung them on the hook next to her deep, clawfoot bathtub.

As the hot water filled the tub, a calm rhythm of a Native American style flute permeated the room bringing her into a serene state of deep relaxation. She could use all the help she could find tonight. It had been a stress-filled few weeks, and she could feel rock-like tension in her neck and shoulders.

Sophie dimmed the light and slipped into the tub. Sighing deeply, she tried to clear her mind of the recent news that had been crowding her brain. I'm going to forget about the strip mall and simply know the Universe will take over, she tried to convince herself. Inhaling deeply, she willed her worries away. With each breath, she exhaled slowly and relaxed every part of her body, systematically and purposefully. The heavenly music floated through the room, and the lavender scent worked its magic. Sophie gazed out of the large window and saw the moon adorning the blackened, star-lit sky, *I could stay here forever.*

Thoughts of Sonya and a small bed and breakfast in Sienna came to mind. It was during their buying adventure for Twins Silver Dream. They had booked two small, adjoining rooms on that part of the trip. Each had a private bath, and they vowed afterwards that the next place they lived would indeed have a deep, clawfoot bathtub. "Sonya, you would love my cabin. I miss you so very much," she whispered. As silent tears slowly found their way down her cheeks, she smiled and thought about Ruthie Louise and breathed, "I felt your heartbeat, Sonya."

Then, as an afterthought, *Jacob Higgins is coming over tomorrow night. I know you'll be here with me.*

Sophie glanced at her prunish fingertips, a sign to leave the now tepid water and dry off. She left the water in the tub, pulled on her comfy PJs, and hoped the soothing lavender would ease her into a restful night's sleep.

Opening the curtains in her bedroom to the peaceful night sky, Sophie contemplated the loveliness before her. Though extremely cold outside, from inside her cozy cabin, the beauty took her breath away. She loved her home and wanted nothing more than to simply enjoy this quiet forever.

Jacob

It's Friday, and Jacob is coming to dinner, Sophie thought as soon as the sun peaked in the window and nudged her awake. *If only I can convince him that selling his childhood homestead to that awful company is a horrible idea.*

Sophie hadn't mentioned to anyone that she reached out to Jacob. She didn't want to buoy up her friends, just in case the meeting was a big disappointment.

Thinking that empathy could play a part of her scheme, Sophie listed names of local shops in her journal. She knew at least a few were in business way back when Jacob lived in the big brick house. *Would it make a difference to him?* she wondered.

After coffee, she bundled up and headed out to

her labyrinth. *It's been way too long since I've spent time here,* Sophie mused. As she slowly walked the circular path, she reflected on the evening ahead.

I'm going to be honest and open with Jacob and see what happens. He's been away for so long; maybe he hasn't even thought about the community consequences. I honestly think he's forgotten there are people involved and small family businesses at stake, Sophie thought to herself.

Later that day, as she started prepping the dinner, Sophie remembered suddenly that she had forgotten to text Jacob her address. *Well, I can't persuade him, if he doesn't even know where I live,* she chuckled to herself. *I'll text him as soon as I finish making the salad.*

The menu also included her favorite comfort foods, shrimp and grits and southern-style biscuits. The shrimp recipe came from a small restaurant in New Orleans. Through the years, she tweaked it a bit and added caramelized onions and extra shrimp. She loved to cook, but liked to improvise with recipes.

Arugula salad was already made and in the refrigerator. *A healthy side dish is always a plus. We can add the lemon vinaigrette when it's served.* She went a little overboard and knew she'd be having leftover salad for days afterwards.

For dessert she made chocolate cupcakes with

a Reese's cup in the center. Joszette, an accomplished baker, shared the decadent recipe with her years ago. Sophie had gotten out the pastry bag and made the peanut butter frosting swirled and fancy. *Who knows, maybe I'll become a pastry chef one day?* she chuckled. In a surprisingly good mood, Sophie considered the task she was undertaking in a few short hours.

On the way upstairs, she smiled at Sonya's portrait and headed to her bedroom.

She found her phone on her nightstand, realizing that she had missed a few messages. One from Amanda said, "Tony is so upset. He wants to yell at somebody over this mess. I'm afraid his blood pressure is sky high, so I'm trying to calm him down. We will see you at the meeting tomorrow afternoon."

Bryan also texted saying, "We have made a petition to stop the sale, and everyone in town will be signing it tomorrow." His message ended with, "It can't hurt to try."

It was only a few hours before Jacob was due to arrive. Everything was ready. She sent off a quick text with her address, "22 Winding Stream Lane, Duck Creek." Sophie put her phone back on the nightstand.

Ginger was sleeping under a chair as Sophie set the table, decorating with a pretty pile of fragrant pine cones gathered after walking earlier.

Her hand-woven basket overflowed with the pine-cones' fragrance, reminding her of her treasured woods. A handful of holly branches adorned with bright red berries punctuated the display. "Perfect," she admitted as she set the basket in the center of the table and pulled out wine glasses, setting them next to the tall water goblets.

Earlier, Sophie did a search on Google to decide on what wine would be best for her meal. It was a white wine, called Viognier, similar to chardonnay. It was described online. *This wine will bring out the natural, caramelized sweetness of the onions, while adding a lovely, crisp floral character that compliments the spices beautifully.* "Alright, this is the one," she said after reading the fancy narrative. Luckily, the local wine shop had it in stock when she stopped by the day before.

Nearly ready, Sophie opened up her top dresser drawer to pick out jewelry for the evening. She was wearing a long, basic black dress that loosely flowed over her hips, hoping it gracefully camouflaged the weight that she kept gaining. She had noticed lately that her clothes were getting snug, yet loved her curves and was content with what she saw in the mirror.

Sophie decided on a lovely pendant crafted with a smooth green gemstone called fuchsite. It reminded her of malachite, one of Sonya's favorites. They had been experts in suggesting the perfect stone for customers looking for natural inspiration. She instantly recalled what she repeated to countless customers over the years, *Fuchsite is a gemstone for comprehension. It speaks to the mind and heart together, helping you and others to use emotions and logic as a combined force.* Sophie rolled her shoulders and relaxed, *This will help Jacob understand why he can't possibly let a strip mall be built on his land.* She kept her jewelry simple, reminding herself this was really a business meeting and not a date.

Her thoughts bolted back to the present moment when a loud, almost angry pounding on the door broke her thoughts. Ginger dashed under the bed, where she would most likely stay until their guest was long gone. Taking another deep breath, Sophie held her pendant in her hand and walked out to the living room.

She opened the door, and there stood Jacob with fist raised, about to punish the door again. His other hand clasped a bottle of wine, still in the brown paper bag, all wrinkled at the top from his firm grip.

He was taller than she remembered, as she looked up to see his face. His features were frozen into a sneer, as he lowered his arm. She stood there a second, confused. "Please come in, Jacob," she offered as she regained her composure. "I'm happy that you could make it on such short notice." She observed he was stiff and appeared uncomfortable.

Sophie moved to the side to allow him to enter. As he glanced around, he relaxed, and remarked, "This place is like an art gallery!"

Sophie was so preoccupied with her lists, and whatnot, she completely forgot about her home and the reaction most had when they first entered. His attitude was childlike, as his eyes got big, taking it all in. "Where did all these statues and sculptures come from?" he asked in awe. "You've done some major traveling. Very impressive," he said shyly. "I've been meaning to plan some trips, but it's kind of never happened."

Sophie was only half listening, distracted with her thought, *Jacob is gorgeous!*

He was tall with dark wavy hair, a little longer than she remembered. His deep mesmerizing brown eyes flecked with hints of gold. He was casually dressed in a navy-colored polo and worn jeans. *My, those faded jeans look good on him,* trying hard not to stare.

"Here, let me take your coat, Jacob," she said, suddenly feeling timid.

He seemed to regain his self-control and stated, "I almost didn't come over tonight. You deceived me."

"What do you mean, deceived you? I just invited you over. That's all," Sophie replied.

"I've had a difficult few months, with my dad being sick and passing away. When you called, it was a reprieve from my worries. I was looking forward to catching up and spending the evening with you. I thought about our conversation throughout the week, and each time it made me smile. Then...you sent me your address," he hesitated but continued, "I realized all at once, like a ton of bricks, actually, that you had an agenda. You live in Duck Creek and your only interest is the notice at city hall of my property sale. You intentionally duped me."

Sophie moved towards the living room where the fire was dwindling. She motioned for Jacob to have a seat, while she added a few more logs. "Let me explain," she said quietly as her hand once again found the smoothness of the gemstone pendant.

They sat quietly, both staring into the fire for a few minutes, as she gathered her thoughts. From outside in the woods there was a distinct *hoot*.

"What was that?" Jacob questioned.

"Oh, a great horned owl. He's giving his territorial call. They're nocturnal, so he's probably just waking up. I hear him about this time most nights. I named him Darius, she admitted. You know, from Hootie & the Blowfish?"

Jacob laughed at the name. "You're hilarious, Sophie. I guess it's been a long time since I've been out in the country like this. It is so quiet you can hear the owls. I used to ride into town with my mom on Wednesdays when she had her hair done. We would come home about dinner time and the owls would be hooting. It's funny how I forgot all about that until just now."

"Did your mom go to Citrine's Hair Salon? inquired Sophie.

"Yes, that's the one," Jacob replied. Sophie watched Jacob's warm eyes soften as he brought back memories of his mother. She also noticed how his wide shoulders filled out the casual polo shirt he was wearing.

Sophie poured wine in the glasses as the flames flickered in the fireplace. Each bringing their glasses to their lips.

Getting up her nerve, Sophie continued the conversation. "Citrine Hair Salon will be closing down soon. It's a shame, because Miss Laurie, the owner, is Casey's aunt, "Sophie explained. "Casey is the only one in their family who's gone to college and her aunt has been footing the tuition bill. Casey won't be able to finish her degree when Citrine closes."

"Casey was just a little girl back when I went

to the salon with my mom." Jacob replied.

She noticed Jacob had moved a bit closer to her on the couch, but she didn't mind at all. "Why are they closing?" Jacob asked.

"You probably don't want to hear this, but it's about the impending strip mall. Hair Cuttery will probably be on the list of occupants. A small town beauty shop can't compete. I haven't heard if Bryan's Cafe will be able to stay open, either. Then, there's Daniel's Hardware and a few other family-owned businesses that will be shutting down," Sophie explained in a matter-of-fact tone.

"It's interesting they managed to survive the pandemic because the community pulled together and supported one another," Sophie added. "It was a challenge, and some towns folks are still struggling with paying off the loans," she held her breath, waiting for a response from Jacob.

He sat thoughtfully and then inquired, "Is this the only reason you invited me out here?"

"I didn't invite you to hear the sob stories, exactly. But, I was wondering if you had any idea of the impact the strip mall will have on the community. The place where you grew up will be forced to change drastically. I'm hopeful I can simply shed some light on the situation. That's all." Sophie was honest, as she selected her words carefully and kept her voice gentle, trying to remember to breathe.

Then, as if on cue, they heard the great horned owl again. "And, of course it's not just about people. With the forest decimated, there will be a significant impact on the wildlife that make their home among the trees," she added with a frown.

Not wanting to let her spontaneous frown spoil the mood, she jumped up from the couch and moved towards the kitchen, motioning for him to follow. "Let's go into the kitchen. Dinner is almost ready."

Carrying their empty glasses, the aroma of the spicy shrimp drifted through the air. "Umm, something smells wonderful," Jacob noted. Sophie finished up the last-minute preparations and placed their plates on the table, along with enough salad to feed ten people. He chuckled and mentioned, 'You were expecting me to eat enough for an army?" he questioned with an amused grin.

"I hope you are hungry," Sophie tried to sound cheerful. "I love to cook, especially when I have company. I also love to eat!" she stated.

Between the fire, wine, and dinner, Sophie and Jacob mellowed markedly from the angry knocking. The easy manner she noticed on the phone with Jacob had once again returned.

"I used to collect rocks when I was little," said Jacob, mainly from the creek in the backyard.

When I started cleaning out the house, I found the box, with my hand-printed labels. One reminded me of your gemstone jewelry. It was labeled a geode."

"Geodes are usually very sparkly," said Sophie. Her voice softened to barely a whisper, "Sonya loved gems that sparkled."

Sophie stood up without saying a word, opened another bottle of wine, and refilled their glasses. They were sitting back in the living room, quietly content and comfortable. The few moments of silence seemed natural and not awkward at all.

"I love watching the flames flicker; they are hypnotic," remarked Jacob. "I'd love to have an outdoor fire pit one day. It would feel like camping. My dad and I used to sleep in a tent next to the creek during the summer, sometimes."

Sophie instinctively reached up and caressed her gemstone pendant and smiled in reply.

Ginger padded down the stairs and joined them in the living room. She meowed softly to make her presence known and greeted Sophie by gently rubbing and snuggling against her legs. "I'm surprised she came out," laughed Sophie. The usually-shy cat then made her way over to Jacob and pretty much demanded he scratch behind her ears, as only cats can.

"She is so friendly. She must sense how much I love animals," said Jacob, as he enjoyed the attention nearly as much as Ginger.

"How's your Twins Silver Dream store?" Jacob asked, not picking up on Sophie's melancholy tone earlier.

"I closed the shop and moved out here after Sonya died," she stated bluntly, but instantly regretted her choice of words. Sophie dropped her face into her hands and whimpered. She was momentarily incapable of moving, or continuing.

Jacob wrapped his strong arms around her, and they stayed that way until Sophie regained her calm. Her deep brown eyes were glazed, and one tear slowly slid down her cheek.

Sophie felt startlingly secure in Jacob's embrace and didn't want it to end. She was torn, as she had lately been in full control over her emotions when it came to Sonya. It had been a while since a man had comforted her, and she relished the solid physical contact of one so undeniably handsome.

"Sonya passed away a few years ago, from the coronavirus," she told Jacob softly. "I had no desire to keep our jewelry store open without her. It's been really hard, but now I'm mostly comfortable and recovering. The cabin is truly my sanctuary, and I'm making a life out here in Duck Creek. It's peaceful, and the forest is good for my soul."

Jacob held her a little while longer, both lost in thought, but remaining silent.

Sophie's cuckoo clock, a relic from one of her many traveling adventures, chimed midnight. "I didn't realize it was so late," she remarked.

"I'd better get going," said Jacob reluctantly letting go as he stood up, towering over her.

No more was said about the shopping mall. Jacob's anger had dissipated as the pleasant evening progressed. They walked out onto the porch together, with the crisp cold air being a complete contrast to the warmth and glow of Sophie's cozy living room. Glancing up at the same time, they gazed at the clear dark sky twinkling with stars and a bright, silver moon.

"I honestly love it here," said Sophie, as she hugged herself to keep warm.

"I'd forgotten how dark and quiet it is in these woods," replied Jacob.

"I'll be right back," she suddenly declared as she ran into her cabin.

He stood there, alone on her porch, listening to the night sounds, including the owl once again. There was a porch swing piled with blankets on one side and a wood pile with old, worn-out leather gloves on top over next to the railing. He noticed a few leftover pottery planters scattered around, with remnants of fall plants, long wilted with the cold.

Holly bushes with bright red berries adorned both sides of the wide, welcoming steps, which he had pounded up, without a second glance, just a few short hours ago.

"Sorry, I know it's cold out here," she said as she handed him a plate wrapped up in foil. "We never had dessert," she smiled. "It's my favorite part of the meal! Actually, Sonya and I used to eat dessert first, sometimes," she admitted. Jacob laughed and gladly took the plate from her outstretched arm.

Sophie shared one last story. "Sonya and I went to Italy. It was our last trip together, but will always be a happy memory. It was planned so we could buy jewelry for Twins Silver Dream, and of course we found lots of jewelry for ourselves, too. It was amazing," she said dreamily. "Near the end of the adventure, we were talking about all the delicious desserts and how we would miss the artistry of the superior pastry chefs. We decided to make a few meals all about sweets and wine. Oh, we had a fabulous time. We even bought matching spoons engraved with, "Always have dessert first."

Sophie laughed and remarked, "Dessert also makes an awesome breakfast."

Jacob smiled as he headed to his car.

A Breakfast Cupcake

The next morning, with Ginger still buried under the covers, Sophie awoke to a rooster from Amanda and Tony's farm announcing the morning.

Last night's dream was slightly different than usual. She saw Sonya and herself as young, teen girls. It was like she was watching an old home movie, featuring her and her beloved sister.

They were baking something chocolatey together during the cooler months of autumn. The air was brisk with a flurry of colorful leaves swirling around, but it was cozy inside the small kitchen of her childhood.

"Do we really have to measure everything?" Sonya said as she dumped in the third cup of flour.

"Uh-oh, the ingredients said two cups of flour. We can make adjustments because baking is like science," explained Sophie, who was obviously the one with higher math skills.

Although when it was time to add the chocolate chips, they both agreed, "More is better!" Needless to say, they enjoyed an abundance of cookies when they were finished in the kitchen that day.

With the dream still in her thoughts and coffee in hand, Sophie remembered her idea to write Ruthie Louise a thank you letter. It had been way too long since her visit and shocking news of Sonya's organ donation.

Sophie gathered a notecard, a favorite pen, and headed back to bed. She snuggled under the covers with pillows propped up against the headboard. The pen was hand-carved from a variety of beautiful hardwoods and polished smooth. *I bought this for myself years ago at Sage and Thyme. It was made by a local wood-craftsman, Mike. I wonder if he's still making these special pens? Maybe I'll send one to Ruthie Louise some day,* Sophie smiled as she recalled the quaint shop and her dear friends, Leya and Tommy. "I really hope they don't have to close the store," she said to Ginger.

Ginger stretched and purred as Sophie wrote a heartfelt note. "I guess you are tired this morning, Miss Social Butterfly," said Sophie, referring to her shy cat's surprise appearance during her dinner with Jacob the evening before. She scratched behind Ginger's ears, as the kitty showed appreciation by snuggling closer.

Sophie went into the kitchen with her empty coffee mug to find a stamp. She refilled her mug and decided, "Dessert does make an awesome breakfast," as she selected a beautifully decorated cupcake from under the cake dome. "I wonder if Jacob is also eating a peanut butter cupcake for breakfast?"

She sat down at the table and sipped the steaming coffee as her mind drifted to the meeting being held at Town Hall later in the afternoon. If Jacob was determined to sell to Smith & Sons Development, she hoped the petitions overflowing with signatures would make a difference. "I'm not the only one that will give them a piece of my mind," Sophie said aloud as she thought of her friend Amanda.

Amanda and her husband Tony lived the simple life and were happy depending on the land they loved for their livelihood. Tony supplied local restaurants, like Bryan's Cafe, with fresh produce. The goats they raised were used to make goat cheese and Amanda's special soap and lotions. *Amanda loves those goats,* Sophie thought. She giggled to herself as she remembered Amanda mentioning, yoga with baby goats. Now that would be entertaining to watch. And, of course, Amanda's goat's milk soap was one of Sophie's favorites.

Sophie brought herself back to the moment, took a big bite of the cupcake, and opened the address book. Tucked inside was the envelope given to her by Ruthie Louise. She opened the envelope. Ruthie Louise's mailing address was written on a plain white index card.

Also included with the mailing address was a cashier's check made out to Sophia Walker. The amount was significant. A gasp escaped her lips and she nearly choked on the cupcake. Blinking her eyes, Sophie examined the check to be sure she was seeing correctly. She counted the string of zeros trailing the number written on the check. It was more money than she had ever earned in all the years of co-owning the boutique, Twins Silver Dream. Sophie sat in stunned silence, her eyes wide with amazement.

Walking in Sunshine

I *need to walk in the woods,* she thought urgently as her buzzing mind whirled in different directions. She started marching towards the trees, without realizing how quickly she was moving. Her need to be among the trees was particularly strong. Her coat blew open and she wrapped it tightly, intentionally slowing her stride slightly, trying to even her breathing. The dappled sunshine didn't add much warmth, but it somehow made her dwell on nature, instead of the thoughts crowding her brain.

Sophie ignored the beeps her cellphone was making in her pocket. *I'll see everyone soon enough at the meeting. There's no sense aggravating myself unnecessarily,* she thought as she dipped under a branch. She meandered through the tall trees and stopped every few minutes, reveling in the sunshine. She lifted her face towards the sun and just let the rays do their magic. *Makes me think of one of Sonya's favorite quotes...*

> *Keep your face to the sun and you*
> *will never see the shadows.*
> ~ **Helen Keller**

The ground was soft with leaves and she tread carefully, except for the occasional crunch of a branch in her path. Sophie heard a woodpecker in the distance and saw the bright flash of red, knowing a cardinal landed right above her. It's a cardinal couple, one bright, the mate a duller color, and they seemed to waltz as they frolicked through the branches. Leya, her friend from the shop in town, liked to remind Sophie, "When you see a cardinal, it means a loved one is visiting." Sophie chuckled and remarked, "I wonder what it means if you see two cardinals dancing?" she asked a squirrel who scurried by.

Sophie slackened her pace, gathering small branches for kindling as she walked. *I believe I'd like to have Jacob over again,* she thought and smiled as she recalled his arms embracing her by the fire. Her daydreams were wandering in an unexpected direction where Jacob was concerned. Sophie inwardly admitted she felt a sensual stir last night, being so close to Jacob. *I'm being ridiculous. He was simply trying to comfort me. That's all,* she thought logically.

Once the distracting thoughts were under control, she thought about the meeting. *Does Jacob truly understand the situation of selling his land to a greedy developer? Will anything I told him last night make a difference?* she contemplated. *What amount of money is being negotiated for the property? Is it now possible for me to outbid the developer?*

By the time she reached the edge of the stream, close to the open field, her arms were very full, and she was tired. Sophie's mind kept returning to the idea of purchasing the Higgin's land. "I'll come back for these later," she told herself as she dropped the branches in a big heap.

Sophie sat on a big rock with her old worn leather gloves and tall boots keeping her warm. The sun streamed through the trees, dancing in designs on the ground. *When it gets warmer, I AM going to put in the swing that Amanda suggested. Maybe I'll install two, so there's plenty of space to share,* she thought excitedly. The water in the creek glinted with bright sparkles and splashed on the rocks. "I love being here," she said aloud with genuine passion.

Cockwombles

Jacob had driven home from Sophie's with a grin on his face. He ate one of the scrumptious cupcakes as soon as he pulled out of her yard. "This is heavenly," he moaned aloud. Jacob turned up John Denver on the radio as he rounded a county road. With no traffic this late at night, he made it home quicker than driving out to the cabin earlier. *Duck Creek really is not that far away*, he concluded.

Once home, Jacob's dog, Dudley, greeted him with urgency. He did a little "I have to pee dance" with an added "Why did you leave me for so long?" thrown in for good measure. Jacob quickly put on Dudley's leash and took him for a brisk stroll through the small backyard and down the path to an open field behind his property. There, he let his dog off the leash, who immediately ran in circles around Jacob's feet. "Sorry, buddy, no playing ball tonight. It's way too late and I'm exhausted." Dudley seemed to understand completely.

Jacob's night was restless. He tossed and turned, accidently kicking his innocent dog, resulting in disgruntled growls from the low-keyed golden retriever curled at the bottom of his bed. Sophie had given him a lot to consider. He knew in only a few short hours he was meeting with his lawyer and owners of Smith and Sons Development to sign the paperwork. This meeting would make it official; his childhood home would be gone forever. He had also promised to attend the town hall meeting later in the afternoon to answer questions. Mayor Dave used to be a close friend of his dad, so Jacob felt obligated when he was personally requested to be present.

Sophie got him thinking about growing up in Duck Creek. Remembering the occasional camping and fishing with his dad outside brought back other memories.

"Having your hands in the soil will make you feel grounded," Jacob's mom always reminded him as they planted the garden each year. As a little boy, he felt grown up planting side by side with his mom. He had experienced a sense of accomplishment, especially when the garden began to flourish and they brought the vegetables to the farmers market to sell. The garden featured neat rows of tall tomatoes in bamboo cages, with shorter curling vines of cantaloupe, and wispy green tops of carrots. Marigolds surrounded the garden. His mom liked to explain, "They're a deterrent for the bunnies and add a splash of color."

In his mind, his mom wore her faded overalls, well-worn work boots, and a silly hat made of straw that she had decorated for a May Day Fair one year. She covered it in silk flowers and ribbons, like an old-fashioned Easter bonnet. Mom insisted on wearing it to protect her hairdo, and it brought fits of giggles from Jacob and his dad every time, without fail. "We must have a picture somewhere," he thought. He also remembered with a sigh, *That hat of hers became old and floppy after years, but she never considered a new one. We even worked in the garden when it was raining,* he mused.

Jacob remembered his mom saying, "You won't melt, Jacob" She always added, "The garden is a brighter shade of green in the rain, with the gift of liquid magic." He dearly missed both his mom and dad.

Dudley was up and expecting his morning walk. "Okay, buddy, we'll make up for your short walk last night."

Once showered and dressed, Jacob was ready to head out to the meeting with the lawyer. "I think I'll take a cup of coffee with me. It's going to be a long day," he said to Dudley. He brightened slightly when he realized he had four more cupcakes left from the dinner with Sophie the evening before. "She's right -- dessert does make a wonderful breakfast."

Jacob noticed it was bright and sunny, and signs of an early spring were all around. Purple and yellow crocuses peeked up at him near his front steps. Bunches of bright yellow and white daffodils lined his fence. *Mom celebrated when the daffodils started blooming,* he recalled. She believed that when you see the yellow faces of daffodils, winter is nearly over.

Pulling into the driveway of the neat, white clapboard house, which was his lawyer's office, Jacob found himself lost in his thoughts. Ms. Ginsburg had been the family attorney for as long as he could remember. She handled their wills and financial issues. Now, her daughter, Clare, was also a partner in the practice. Ms. Ginsberg used to hint to his parents at the possibility of Clare and Jacob getting to know each other on a more intimate level.

It was a small town, so between Jacob's successful architectural business and personal dealings, he was currently one of her major clients. Ms. Ginsburg was slight in stature, but a dynamo in the courtroom. She once disputed a legal matter with one of his structures, having to do with a complex design and an incompetent construction company. She blew him away with her knowledge and expertise. "She's definitely an attorney you want on your side," he admitted to his colleagues after winning the case hands down.

Jacob arrived before the representatives from Smith & Sons, and was greeted by Clare, who he hadn't seen since he was a teenager. She was at least a foot taller than her petite mom. It was hard not to notice her red suit and slim, long legs. Her wavy, black hair swayed in harmony with the background music as she led him into the office. He smiled, straightened his back slightly, but felt a little too casual in his jeans and white button-down shirt.

Ms. Ginsburg stood as he entered her office and came around the desk for a hug, up on her tiptoes. "How are you doing, Jacob?" she asked, remembering the last time they met in person was after his dad passed away, less than a year ago.

He bent way over, still not closing the big gap in their heights. "It's been a challenging few months," he replied.

They only had a few moments of pleasantries, before a commotion interrupted the waiting area. A cell phone rang, and a man's loud voice could be heard answering, "I don't have time for this. Call my secretary on Monday." The door banged several more times, and it sounded like a whole group was arriving.

"Clare, would you please show them to the conference room?" asked Ms. Ginsburg. "It sounds like they brought the whole legal team, and it will be too crowded in here."

Clare walked towards the group, and an older, heavyset man gave a low whistle, rudely directed at her. She abruptly stopped, gave him "the look," and gestured for them to follow her. She noticed that he smiled smugly, along with a few of the others, and she decided they weren't worth her slightest attention.

Once all seated, Ms. Ginsburg mentally noted that they were all overweight white men pompously dressed in dark, wrinkly suits.

Jacob was confused as he whispered to Clare, "What the damn hell?! Why are there six men here to sign one property contract?"

"I hope they don't give mom any problems, or they won't know what hit them," Clare said so only Jacob could hear. She sat down in between Jacob and her mom, to listen, support, and learn from the expert.

Without even waiting for introductions, the same boorish man that whistled at Clare started passing around a stapled sheaf of papers. "We've made some slight adjustments to the development, but it shouldn't affect the sale. It is what it is. Let's get this agreement signed."

Another surly developer, smelling like cigarette smoke, spoke up, "More bang for the buck." Jacob had no idea what he was talking about, as he didn't offer any explanation with his offhand comment.

"We added a five-floor parking garage to make room for all the gamblers at the casino," loudy boasted a pasty-looking younger guy. "Business will be booming by this time next year, for sure. Those good for nothing Mexicans better work fast." His eyes were dull, and his speech jittery, like he had consumed way too much caffeine.

Jacob stood up, nearly knocking his chair over, "Nobody said anything about a casino!"

"Why do you care about what we are building? You'll still get your money," spoke up the whistler, who seemed to be the owner, the rudest and loudest of them all. He was idly playing with a golf ball, like an adolescent with a fidget toy.

Everyone turned as they watched Jacob walk out of the room and slam the door behind him. He rushed into the waiting room, with both Clare and his attorney, Ms. Ginsburg, following closely behind. Jacob slumped into the overstuffed chair in the corner and put his head in his hands with an exasperated sigh.

They could hear several of the men talking

over each other in a heated debate. It sounded like they all left their phones on, and buzzing and beeping interrupted the space.

"I just can't go through with it," Jacob admitted. He let out a gasp, not realizing he had been holding his breath since the boisterous group invaded the quiet. Jacob inhaled slowly, exhaled again, looked at the women, and saw the relief on their faces.

Ms. Ginsburg stated, "It's a challenge for me to deal with cockwombles, but a whole room full of them?"

Clare hissed, "Loud, narcissistic, racist, misogynistic chauvinists!"

All three relaxed slightly, grinned, and listened briefly to the commotion going on behind the closed door.

"Jacob, go ahead and leave. I'll take care of the situation here," Ms. Ginsburg soothed compassionately.

Jacob noticed Clare smiling at him as he turned towards the door. She asked, "Will I see you at the town hall this afternoon?" He just nodded and moved towards the exit. It was as if a huge weight lifted from his shoulders, and he felt the tension melt away as he got into his car.

Town Hall Hullabaloo

"Oh, my gosh, look at all these cars," said Amanda to Tony as they pulled into town.

"I didn't know we had this many people in Duck Creek," Tony added.

They were able to squeeze the truck into an empty spot on the grassy area where the Farmers Market resided in the warmer months. As they made their way towards city hall, cars lined up along Main Street, filling every spot.

The weather had turned a corner and the freshness of spring was in the air. They strolled arm-in-arm down the sidewalk. The murmur of voices welcomed them as the large ornate doors opened at the top of the steps.

On her previous visit to town, Amanda and

Sophie heard the dreadful news of the property sale from Leya, the owner at Sage and Thyme.

Daniel Hernandez and his son, Pete, were the first friends they saw. "How do you like the new chicken coop?" Daniel, the owner at the hardware store, asked. Tony had shared Amanda's vision of the small, dollhouse-looking structure with him. Daniel was able to suggest the supplies needed to make her image come to life. It even had the tiny windows and flower boxes she wanted.

Next, they saw Casey with her Aunt Laurie. Casey had been Amanda's neighbor when she lived in town. Casey looked as though she'd been crying, and her pretty green eyes were bloodshot and red. "Come here, my dear girl" Amanda folded her young friend in a tender hug.

Tony had moved on and could be seen shaking hands with Bryan. "Can you and Amanda add your names to these petitions, please? This one is for business owners, and the one Tommy is holding is for residents. You qualify to sign both, as do most of us here today," he stated in a businesslike manner.

Miss Laurie and Casey excused themselves to go to the ladies room, in hopes that a splash of cold water would help Casey get her emotions in check. She struggled so at balancing her college classes and working. She was heartbroken that it might all have to end. "All because of some high and mighty businessmen who want to open a stripmall!" exclaimed Miss Laurie, who owned and operated the salon, Citrine. Her Aunt Laurie financed her tuition. The stability of Citrine Hair Salon was now in jeopardy due to the stripmall plans.

Brenda and Lori entered the large room holding hands. They seemed very surprised at how many people were gathered. Their Novel Book Shoppe had been visited by practically every single person in the crowd. Lori had a knack for choosing books that fit the personality of customers and said to Leya, "We have a new book on essential oils that I think you'll appreciate. It specializes in blends with jasmine, sweet basil, and lavender, your favorites."

Casey came out of the ladies room with Miss Laurie, Devin, and Lily. Devin and Lily were lifesavers to Sonya and Sophie back when they traveled to Italy. They went from working part-time to running the business when the twins were away. Devin was wearing sterling dangle earrings that caught the light and twinkled as sunshine streamed through the large windows of the hall. Her long, blonde hair shone, as she tucked it behind her ear. Lily, whose skin was the color of caramel, had on a large, iridescent moonstone that glowed against her smooth skin. "I can't believe this is all happening," Devin said sadly.

With the help of Tommy, Bryan circulated, having everyone sign the petitions. The pages filled up quickly.

The crowd was loud as more neighbors joined. If it wasn't for the disturbing situation, it would have been a reunion. The harsh winter kept everyone indoors, yet there was the expectation of spring and warmer weather. Many neighbors hadn't seen each other in a few months, except maybe for a brief conversation over the produce aisle at the market, or a quick lunch at Bryan's Cafe.

Paul, the owner of the large building currently occupied by Bryan's Cafe, came in with Mayor Dave. They milled through the group, shaking hands and greeting old friends.

Mayor Dave was ready to get the meeting started when Sophie arrived. She walked in with an air of confidence, wearing her dress jeans and short black boots. She had on a soft velvet burn-out blazer in black and gold. It was a splurge from a mail-order catalogue, Coldwater Creek. The long, tailored jacket flowed enticingly as she walked. She had applied sheer lip gloss before getting out of her car. *I suppose Jacob will be here today. A little added shine can't hurt,* she said as she glanced in the rearview mirror.

Amanda immediately went over and gave her

friend a long hug. In the last week, they had spent hours discussing this mess, but now no words were needed. Amanda slipped two small candy bars into Sophie's hand, "for energy," she quickly whispered with a wink. Sophie looked down and saw a Mounds bar and Almond Joy bar, her and her sister's favorites.

Sophie's mind drifted briefly back in time to Sonya. Sonya always had a chocolate treat to share during times of stress.

The sharp rap of the gavel brought Sophie back. Mayor Dave was up front, trying to get everyone to quiet down, so the meeting and question and answer session could begin. Sophie was still standing next to Amanda when she glanced up front. There she saw Jacob, taller than just about everyone, standing very close to a stunning woman she did not recognize. The unidentified woman was wearing a red cashmere sweater with pearls. Her long, wavy hair was impressive, and she looked up at Jacob with her radiant smile. Sophie noticed she had her hand rested on his arm, in a familiar, but more than friendly manner.

Amanda muttered, "That must be Jacob Higgins next to Dave. I don't see anybody that could be representatives from the development company, do you?" Sophie was distracted and didn't reply.

Neighbors were starting to settle down, as

Tony found his way back to Amanda and Sophie. "Smith & Sons aren't here," he declared with disappointment.

The hardwood gavel echoed in the hall three times, and everyone hushed. The mayor formally welcomed everyone and once again stated the reason for the meeting. The noise level started going up again, as Bryan strode towards the podium, holding the petitions.

"May I speak before you go further?" Jacob interrupted, looking serious, but still very relaxed and handsome. Sophie noticed all eyes on Jacob, especially the woman, but in a different kind of way. Mayor Dave handed him the microphone.

Jacob appeared concerned, yet still managed to look at ease. Sophie's heart fluttered. When he made eye contact with her, he smiled and gave a little wave. Her heart did a rhythmic dance that she could not control.

"Good afternoon. My name is Jacob Higgins, and I've known many of you since I was a little boy and fished in Duck Creek. After my dad passed away, I didn't think anything or anyone was left for me here. The memories were just too hard. When I decided to sell, I wasn't thinking straight. When I went back to the house to start clearing things, I missed my mom and dad so much." He had to take a moment to compose himself before he continued. "Then, Sophie called." Heads turned and Sophie felt like she was in a spotlight. "I didn't realize my decision was affecting all the people that live here. After talking with Sophie, I was able to remember the happy times." He paused once again, still smiling across the crowded room at Sophie. "You don't need to hear all the details, but I didn't sign the agreement. I'm no longer selling the homestead where I grew up."

Whoops of cheer and applause reverberated powerfully through the hall! Hugging and tears of joy took over each group of friends.

Baffled, Sophie blinked, unable to completely comprehend the current situation. Jacob suddenly appeared next to her and placed his arm protectively around her shoulder. They looked at each other, as the room faded. Jacob murmured, "You're absolutely right, dessert does make an awesome breakfast."

Because You Can

One brilliant autumn morning, Sophie woke up early. Jacob was asleep next to her with Dudley curled up beside him. "Maybe I should get a bigger bed," she chuckled as he stretched and woke up. Jacob stayed at her house during the renovations to his old family home, and she was kind of getting used to having him around. He traveled some, between his east and west coast architectural firm offices, but was able to take some time off to oversee the construction, which of course he designed.

Sophie fixed herself a cup of coffee and let Dudley out to roam the newly-fenced yard. Ginger spent lots of time in the spare bedroom, where she found solitude away from the large, friendly dog.

Sophie had finally resolved to conquer the jewelry boxes from Italy in the basement. They were delivered and partially forgotten soon after she moved into her cabin. Her grief was too fresh at the time to even consider opening them without Sonya.

She went down the steps with her coffee and a pair of scissors and opened each box, slowly unwrapping every piece of jewelry. Sophie took a moment to appreciate each beautiful item. Wrapped in tissue paper, or inside blue and green velvet pouches, the artful jewelry induced sad smiles. "Sonya, it's just not the same without you here with me. We loved opening the new jewels together," she remembered aloud.

Sophie opened the boxes until all the wondrous jewelry was spread out at her feet. Empty boxes and tissue paper littered the floor. It took a long while to get to this point, but it was finally time. Most memories these days about her dear sister were joyful, and she easily shared stories with Jacob with no hint of the sadness that once gripped her spirit in a vice.

Later, Sophie chose her favorites to keep and wear. She also found the special pieces of jewelry she knew in her heart Sonya would favor. She planned to wear these in remembrance of her special sister.

One by one, Sophie invited friends and close neighbors over to give the precious jewelry as gifts. Amanda, of course, was the first. She oohed and aahed and picked out a large, smooth turquoise pendant, earrings, and bracelet. All different jewelry artists, but they coordinated beautifully, without being too matchy-matchy. "I love sharing with you" Sophie declared to her dear friend.

"These remind me of the ring I have from Tony. He purchased it before you and I met," reminded Amanda.

Lori and Brenda, the owners of Novel Book Shoppe, were about to celebrate their 10th wedding anniversary, so Sophie shared several amazing necklaces with them. As they browsed, their fur babies played happily with Dudley. The pups kept busy ripping up tissue paper on the other side of the nearly empty basement. Brenda and Lori preferred vintage looking pieces, so the necklaces adorned with deep garnet and sapphire gemstones fit them just right. "Thank you so much for thinking of us," said Brenda excitedly. Lori added, "We will remember you and Sonya each time we wear these gifts"

Clare Martinez, who was now happily married to Ethan, was the next recipient. She had taken over the law offices of her mother, the foreboding Ms. Ginsburg. Her husband, a successful entrepreneur in web design, also had an office in the white clapboard house. He currently assisted Amanda in creating a website to facilitate the sale of her body lotions and soaps.

Clare was amazed at Sophie's cabin. "Your collections are so interesting. I love that you traveled the world to find these treasures." she exclaimed. Sophie took her downstairs, where there was still a large collection of jewelry. "Wow, I wish I could have seen your jewelry store. I'm sure I would have been a frequent customer."

While chatting, Sophie discovered that Clare loved rings, so she encouraged her to pick out a couple. The first was a chunky amethyst set in a wide sterling band. The next ring featured a striped brown jasper with deep golden topaz accents. "Wait, I have a pretty blue topaz ring we picked out in a shop in Umbria I think you'll like," said Sophie. She added it to the small white organza bag and smiled.

Sophie realized sharing her jewelry was an excellent idea. She really missed the joy of watching others find the perfect piece. *Now, it's even better because I'm giving them the jewelry as gifts.*

"Clare and her mom were instrumental in getting me out of the contract when I was about to sell the property. I'll always be indebted to their professionalism and powerhouse law skills," Jacob reminded Sophie often.

Ms. Ginsburg was now retired and content with porch sitting, with a tall glass of lemonade in her steady hands. She kept busy making certain her two granddaughters grew up knowing, "Women belong everywhere that decisions are being made." She encouraged them to be free spirits, but to always speak their minds, especially if they encountered injustice in any form. She was still quite involved with consulting with Clare and the new associate, Jody. Business was growing, and Ms. Ginsburg was proud of the work that was being accomplished, especially in the area of women's equality.

"I think these multi-colored freshwater pearls are perfect for your mom," Sophie exclaimed to Clare. "They are magnificently regal, just like her."

"Here are some child-sized pearls for your little girls, too. They can match their Mimi when they get dressed up," she told Clare.

"Renee and Ann love to be like their Mimi. We will cherish these gifts," proclaimed Clare.

Casey was currently the law clerk and valuable assistant at Clare's busy law office. She intentionally stayed close to where she grew up and planned to remain in the area for the time being. Casey picked out a rainbow of fluorite earrings, bracelets, and rings. "It's so fun sharing the jewelry!" Sophie said with exuberance.

"I'll just wear everything right now." Casey said with delight.

Devin and Lily were absolutely thrilled over the dazzling display of beautiful gems. They loved all the jewelry, and Sophie was extremely generous with the two that helped her in the shop years ago. When they left, they both had enough new jewelry to wear with every outfit." We just can't thank you enough," Lily and Devin gushed in agreement.

Jacob remarked, "I love seeing how happy you are when you share the jewelry with friends. It must have been so fun for you and Sonya to work together at Twins Silver Dream."

"It just seems right to share, and I think my sister would agree," she said as she gave him a long, adoring embrace.

Sophie was content and happy with her life. She truly enjoyed time walking the labyrinth, allowing the mint to grow wild. She still spent hours traipsing through the woods, sometimes alone with her thoughts, sometimes with Jacob or Amanda. Connecting with nature held magical qualities for Sophie. "Whether I'm happy or troubled, being amongst the trees is always where I want to be. Life is good." Sophie enthusiastically stated.

It's time to clean out Sonya's clothes, Sophie decided. She had given a pile to a local thrift store years ago, but stored Sonya's favorites in a big cedar chest, kept in the spare bedroom, but now referred to as Ginger's castle. She hadn't thought about or browsed through the clothes since the day she packed them away.

Being twins, they shared and swapped clothes as teens, but each had grown into their own style as they became adults. Sonya had so many clothes with sparkles and sequins, she mused as she picked up a teal blouse that glittered in the sun coming through the open window.

Sophie chose a few sweaters and jackets she wanted to keep, along with several beautiful scarves from their earlier travels. "I'll finally donate the rest of Sonya's clothes," she declared aloud. She felt a calmness come over her with this decision.

Sophie and Jacob were browsing through Sage and Thyme one hot sunny afternoon, like they did at least once a month these days. On the wall, next to the amazing display of succulent plants that Leya just added, she saw an exhibit of charming paintings. They were created by a well-known local artist whose work was getting acclaim in the art world. Over to the left hung the largest of all the paintings. It was an old oak tree that looked familiar. "I remember Amanda admiring this painting when we came in a long time ago." Her dear friend had shared a heartfelt story of Willie many months ago, after one of their long walks through the woods. Willie had been a tree friend in the yard of Amanda's cottage before she met Tony. Sophie now realized why this particular painting caught her eye. "It's Willie. I'm buying this for her!" she exclaimed.

Sophie had told no one about the generous check she received from Ruthie Louise, the recipient of Sonya's heart through organ donation. A brief note included with the hefty check read, "Please spend this in a way that makes others happy."

Since then she'd contributed to families in need, helped Casey with graduate business law courses, added a screened-in porch at Amanda and Tony's farm, and built an elaborate fire pit behind Jack's renovated homestead. She gave Ms. Ginsburg's old office a face lift, along with various other acts of kindness, large and small. To encourage the community to spend more time together, she had a dozen benches installed throughout town. Each time she visited, she observed folks sitting and chatting.

As Leya was wrapping the oak tree masterpiece in layers of tissue paper, Sophie thought about a Dove chocolate wrapper that was taped to her refrigerator.

It simply said, *Because you can*.

Sophie's Resources

Tina's Salve

1 cup dried dandelions (dry on a towel in a cool
dark place for a couple of days)
½ cup coconut oil
½ cup grapeseed oil
½ cup cup olive oil
1 ounce of beeswax
1 squirt of lavender oil

Combine the dried dandelions with oils and stir
together.

Either put on a sunny windowsill for 2 weeks,
                    or
Use a double boiler and heat through, stirring oc-
casionally.
The oil should turn bright yellow.

Melt the beeswax and add lavender oil. Mix with
the dandelion oil.

Cool slightly and pour into 4 ounce canning jars.

Dandelion salve helps aching joints and improves
chapped and dry skin.

Joszette's Peanut Butter Cupcakes

2 cups cake flour
1 ½ cups sugar
1 ½ teaspoons (8g) baking powder
¼ teaspoon (3g) baking soda
¼ teaspoon (3g) salt
2 sticks butter, softened
3 large eggs
1 cup buttermilk
1 tablespoon vanilla extract
1 bag chopped peanut butter cups
cupcake wrappers

Preheat the oven to 325 degrees.
Put the first five ingredients into the bowl of your mixer.
Mix on low speed for at least 30 seconds to combine.
Add the softened butter mix on low speed just until it looks like coarse sand.
Add the eggs, one at a time, mixing until blended.
Add the vanilla to the 1 cup buttermilk.
With the mixer on lowest speed, gradually pour into the mixer. .
Mix for two minutes. Batter will be fluffy and smooth.

Add an icecream scoop of batter in each of the wrappers.
Add a few pieces of the peanut butter cups into the center of the batter before baking.

Bake at 325 degrees for 12 to 18 minutes.

Joszette's Peanut Butter Frosting

1 ½ cups creamy peanut butter

1 cup salted butter, softened

3 ½ cups confectioners' sugar

3-4 tbsp. milk or water

2 teaspoons vanilla extract

Cream the peanut butter and butter in a medium bowl with an electric mixer.

Add sugar, 3 tbsp. milk, and the vanilla extract. Mix with an electric mixer on low for 1 minute. Increase the speed to medium and mix until well combined and fluffy.

Use a piping bag to frost cupcakes after they are cooled.

Garnish with pieces of peanut butter cups.

Sneak Peek

Whispering Chestnut Tree

Casey arrived at Amanda's farm early in the evening of a beautiful, clear day. Summer was her favorite time of year, especially when the humidity was low, like today. She was dressed in a loose green cotton shirt, and black yoga shorts, with her wavy auburn hair pulled up in a topknot. Amanda greeted her, looking amused, "Thanks for coming early, I could use a hand with rounding up our playful friends."

"I'm happy to help.The babies are frisky today," she noted to Amanda. "Max and Gigi are running around in circles over there. Do you think they know it's Baby Goat Yoga at Chestnut Farm time?"

"I'm still laughing at Gigi. Your facial expression was priceless when she stayed on your back during the plank pose in the session last weekend."

The trendy exercise class is extremely popular, and entertaining for everyone involved. The fresh air, and beauty of the farm is the perfect setting for enjoying outdoor yoga with baby goats.

"I knew the class would be a success." Casey gushed. It's a reprieve from being in my law office wearing heels and a suit all day. Doing yoga with baby goats is a highlight of my week. The goats are so darn cute, jumping all over the place, and burping. Hee hee - It's so much fun!."

Books By This Author

Listen To The Trees

Listen to the Trees is Book 1 of the Tree Hugger Series.

Amanda is a visionary. She's a risk-taker. Her friends admire her for her adventurous spirit. What happens when Amanda is faced with unexpected pandemic fears? With the support of mystical hypnotic opportunities, she manages to transform the fears into opportunities.Read to discover how she creates a second chance for love.Don't be surprised, also, if you suddenly have insatiable cravings for ice cream.It's a love story with some metaphysical twists. A must-read for tree-huggers who have a true appreciation for our natural world.

Made in the USA
Middletown, DE
05 June 2021

41196764R00096